The Siege of Leningrad

The Siege of Leningrad
A World War II Novel

Richard G. Hole

World War II

SYNOPSIS

Heavy artillery had begun firing at the Leningrad outskirts, barely ten kilometers from the front line. The immense city, besieged for several months by the iron divisions of the "Wehrmacht" suffered the continuous hammering of long-range guns, heavy mortars and bombs from "Stukas" and "Heinkels", awaiting the decisive moment in that overwhelming everything in their path, the grenadiers would launch the assault, like an unstoppable wave, demolishing the last defensive redoubts ...

The Siege of Leningrad is a story belonging to the World War II collection, a series of war novels developed in World War II.

THE SIEGE OF LENINGRAD

CHAPTER I

The night was gloomy and cold. Large rain-laden clouds covered the sky, and a pale moon loomed between them, illuminating the intricate labyrinth of trenches and barbed wire at intervals with its ghostly glow. Glowing rockets rose into the air, exploding in yellowish gleams as machine guns rattled and single shots rang out from sentries on their parapets. To Kolpino the artillery thundered since dusk.

Private Fritz Rinner's reddened eyes scanned the darkness. The machine gun of which he was a servant rested beside him, ready to go into action. In front of him, the ground broke into a series of treacherous, grassy hollows, from which the mist rose in wide swaths. Large funnels, caused by the explosion of large-caliber shells, covered the terrain around them. Rinner consulted his luminous dial watch. There was still an hour to go before his relief. An uninterrupted procession of evocations and memories passed through his brain. His eyelids were heavy from the long wakefulness, and he longed for the moment when he could lie down on his hard cot to head off a brief sleep.

To his left came the sound of footsteps approaching through the muddy trench. It was the sergeant, who was walking around his sector inspecting the posts.

"All right" Rinner informed him, being careful not to look away from the front, as that would have earned him a good reprimand from his superior.

"We will have it soon", he replied. Headquarters just informed us that the Wahrenfels patrol is returning tonight, having spent two days in the rear of the enemy lines. They will make their entry precisely from this position. The password will be "Sebastopol". Once identified, you point out the path that exists in the fence to your right. And be very careful with getting confused and throwing a blast at them ... huh, showrenco?

The sergeant walked away, Rinner rolled up the collar of his field coat, and prepared himself for the long wait. The minutes passed slowly. Heavy artillery had begun firing at the Leningrad outskirts, barely ten kilometers from the front line. The immense city, besieged for several months by the iron divisions of the "Wehrmacht" suffered the continuous hammering of long-range guns, heavy mortars and bombs from "Stukas" and "Heinkels", awaiting the decisive moment in that overwhelming everything in their path, the grenadiers would launch into the assault, like an unstoppable wave, knocking down the last defensive redoubts.

It would have been about an interminable half hour when Private Rinner thought he perceived in front of him the unmistakable sound of cautious approaching footsteps. He pricked up his ears, and stood motionless, his nerves tense. After a brief interval of silence, the footsteps were heard closer. The moon had set and visibility was practically nil.

"Tall! "Rinner yelled, stepping behind the machine gun with one finger on the trigger." Who lives...? Password!

"German patrol" answered a voice, and then ": Sevastopol!

"The pass is ten or twelve meters to your left," Rinner warned.

The soldier, undoubtedly on a scouting mission, surveyed the terrain and then drove off to report to the others. In a few minutes, the entire patrol was approaching. The grenadier's shod boots made a dull thud as they hit the hard ground, their hooves gleamed faintly, wounded by the glow of the rockets, and their field gear made a faint jingle, oscillating at their rhythmic pace. The first to jump into the trench was Lieutenant Wahrenfels. They were followed by the corporal and the seven grenadiers and the "feldwebel" covered the rear. Engerling. The lieutenant was tall, slim, and slender. However, under his well-cut tunic, one could see strong and firm limbs. In his energetic and lively face, eyes were bright and full of life, protected by the glass of metal-rimmed glasses. His gestures and his voice denoted the leader capable of dragging his people to the most incredible feats with the sole spur of his overwhelming personality. During the Ukrainian campaign, and at the head of his patrol, he had always been the first to assault the enemy fortifications located at the rear of the front lines, preparing the ground for the units that would later consolidate the action. Endowed with a heart of steel, inaccessible to fear or weakness, his orders cracked in the din of explosions, and the clatter of machine guns and the hum of airplanes, as bullets hissed around him in greedy search for difficult prey. At the command post of the Division, he was regarded as a reckless and audacious leader who could be entrusted with the most difficult missions without fear of failure. He was in possession of a multitude of decorations and wore on his chest the most precious of all: a first-class Iron Cross, obtained during the siege and surrender of a very important armored fortress.

The "feldwebel" Engerling was the kind of professional military man, of uncompromising courage and uncompromising loyalty, capable of the most extraordinary actions without a smirk of mocking contempt on his face, blackened by gunpowder.

The seven grenadiers and their corporal Schäfer formed a compact, disciplined and vigorous group. All of them had been chosen with the greatest care and subjected to extremely harsh tests, before becoming part of that patrol, already famous throughout the Division and whose feats were commented by the troops as something fabulous and legendary. They looked impressive in their high mud-covered boots, their leather-belted tunics, their helmets held to the chin by the chinstrap, and their light and efficient weaponry, consisting of a specially made 'submachine gun', regulation pistol, mango and egg bombs distributed by the belt, and a well-sharpened machete, which they only used in cases of trouble or when it was convenient to eliminate the adversary with the least possible noise.

Those men, used to looking death in the face, never trembled. A disdainful and ironic smile never faded from their lips, while feverishly wielding their weapons, they made their way through the enemy ranks with accurate bursts, or when, like lurking wolves, they spied on the enemy's movements for hours, to launch themselves at the action at the precise moment of sounding the command order.

Among them, three grenadiers stood out for their vigor and personality, whom everyone called the inseparable ones. Their names were Bert Seidel, Alf Voss, and Rudi Main, and they were the cornerstone on which the total organization of the patrol rested. They had been together since the beginning of the campaign and had been chosen by the lieutenant, not only for their extraordinary physical abilities, but also for their easygoing and aggressive character, and for their good humor and cordiality, proof of all adversity. They enjoyed limitless popularity throughout the regiment, and were known as much for their exploits as for their jokes, genius, and daring of all kinds.

Bert Seidel, a former office worker from Munich, was of regular height, but of very strong build and great resistance to fatigue. With a somewhat childish face, she had extremely expressive brown eyes, brown hair and a broad and powerful chest, acquired in the practice of the hardest sports. Alf Voss, had to leave the university classrooms to join a unit that soon left for the front. Somewhat taller than Bert, he looked extremely healthy and spirited. With tanned skin and black eyes, he could have been taken for a Southerner. Yet he came from an old Hannover family, and was characterized by his exquisite upbringing and extremely correct manners. For his part, Rudi, the tallest of the three, was of unusual build. His blue eyes stood out in a face with a prominent jaw, and his robust neck rested on broad, muscular athlete's shoulders capable of supporting the most extraordinary loads. Over his broad forehead, the blond locks of his constantly tousled hair fell. With a lively and penetrating gaze, he possessed an extremely alert intelligence. In his spare time he had devoted himself to the study of Russian, mastering it to perfection, and this constituted an invaluable advantage for the patrol, since on many occasions, a word pronounced in a pure accent of the country, had been more effective than the action of hand bombs or machine pistols. Over his broad forehead, the blond locks of his constantly tousled hair fell. With a lively and penetrating gaze, he possessed an extremely alert intelligence. In his spare time he had devoted himself to the study of Russian, mastering it to perfection, and this constituted an invaluable advantage for the patrol, since on many occasions, a word pronounced in a pure accent of the country, had been more effective than the action of hand bombs or machine pistols. Over his broad forehead, the blond locks of his constantly tousled hair fell. With a lively and penetrating gaze, he possessed an extremely alert intelligence. In his spare time he had devoted himself to the study of Russian, mastering it to perfection, and this constituted an invaluable advantage for the patrol, since on many occasions, a word pronounced in a pure accent of the country, had been more effective than the action of hand bombs or machine pistols.

The lieutenant trusted them completely and completely, and never hesitated to entrust them with the most difficult operations, sure that they would come out with the most terrible tests.

They lined up, and the lieutenant passed them a brief review.

"Everything in order, guys" he told them. Now, to rest, how well deserved we have it ... That is, if they let us.

"I have an idea, my lieutenant" said Rudi, to whom the patrol leader sometimes allowed certain slight familiarities. Why doesn't one of those jerks of the General Staff, who spend their lives planning operations, not accompany us on each of our outings? Maybe that way ...

"An excellent idea" replied the aforementioned, interrupting him. But would you like to spend eight or nine hours a day sitting at a table surrounded by plans and colored pencils? No right? Well, to each his own, Rudi ... And now on the move, that the weather threatens rain.

The patrol started on its way to the command post, trench ahead, and soon disappeared around a bend in it.

CHAPTER II

Old Ivan's tavern was located on the main street of Novo-Litka. The village, made up mostly of wooden "isbas" stretched out on both sides of the main Leningrad-Vilnius road, which the long caravans of trucks that carried out the service between the rear ran tirelessly, day and night. and the front.

The place was the meeting point for the soldiers with permission, who filled it completely at all hours, making the atmosphere unbreathable with the thick smoke of cigarettes and pipes while the noise of the conversations did not cease to be perceived for a single moment.

Katia, the tavern keeper's daughter, circulated among the tables, attentive to the demands of the patrons. She was a tall and slender blonde, with an expressive face, in which splendid blue eyes stood out with an inviting and mischievous expression, and a mouth with plump, red lips, always open in a luminous smile. She was in her early twenties, and her charms attracted and enthralled the local regulars, some of whom gazed at her fresh and inviting beauty with more than just admiration. However, Katia, a girl of foolproof formality, did not allow anyone the slightest lack of respect, even if she had a kind word or a friendly and cordial gesture for everyone.

Alf, Bert and Rudi entered the tavern. They had stripped off their military equipment, and with the warrior's collar unbuttoned, the cap twisted over one ear and the pistol hanging from the belt, the three athletes, tanned by the sun and snow of long campaigns, looked capable. to move how many feminine hearts they will find in their path.

They sat at a table in the center of the room, which was empty at that moment, and briefly observed the crowd. Katia solicitously came to serve them.

"What do you guys want to drink? Asked Bert. Today I am the one who invites.

"For my part, I don't think I'm going to have enough even with a liter of 'vodka'. I have to get the gunpowder taste out of my mouth after our last foray.

Katia, who understood German perfectly, gave Rudi an admiring look, to which he responded by winking and smiling.

"What are you telling me, precious? He asked, taking her by the wrist and adding in perfect Russian:

Monoga krashiva. Lubliets minya?

She slapped him on the neck.

"'Stoj!" "She replied, and then in German, so that everyone would understand." What do these familiarities with me come to? Am I your girlfriend?

"No, but you could be" Rudi answered, pulling her towards him and making a gesture of kissing her.

A group of three tankers watched the scene from the adjoining table. They were tall and strong, with that weathered face and aggressive and tenacious expression that characterized the soldiers of a weapon haloed by the glory of the sweeping advances, the spectacular offensives and the mass attacks, while the cannons spewed shrapnel around their monsters. of steel. They wore the black uniform of his Corps and adorned their characteristic berets with a silver skull, an emblem of courage and contempt for death. Apparently one of them had hitherto enjoyed Katia's preferences, and as he observed Rudi's attitude, he felt a fit of rage wash over him. The rivalry between tankers and infantrymen was traditional in the army, since the former were considered superior to the rest of the troop,

Who is that guy? The tanker grumbled, giving Rudi a hateful look.

The grenadier raised his head sharply and stared at his rival with an expression of restrained calm.

"You think you are a great conqueror, right? "Continued the other, emboldened." Stop bothering that girl!

"I don't think Katia feels bothered by my side" Rudi commented with an ironic smile. At least he shouldn't be looking at a monkey face like yours.

The tanker got up fast as an arrow and, turning to Rudi, he unleashed a punch that he dodged, sending him tumbling against the table. Bottles and glasses fell to the ground. Without giving him time to collect himself, Rudi caught him by the waist and threw him at his two companions. For their part, Bert and Alf were preparing to attack. The tankers gasped in fierce rage. The three grenadiers awaited the mass onslaught of their adversaries with great serenity. Rudi's rival gained momentum and threw himself at him with the intention of smashing him against a wall. But Rudi, trained for a long time in a Berlin gym, knew a good number of keys and holds that now the time had come to apply. Stepping aside at the right moment, he slightly twisted his waist and grabbed the tanker by one arm, He flipped him cleanly over his shoulder, knocking him down on the hard wooden floor, which trembled at the impact. Bert had taken down his enemy and was punching him at will. For their part, Alf and the third tanker were locked in a hand-to-hand fight, in which both received and applied superb blows.

Rudi's opponent jumped to his feet. His face was covered in blood and his uniform was torn in several places. A tremendous direct threw Rudi against the wall. One of the ceiling lamps crashed to pieces. The grenadier flinched as if in terrible pain, and just as the other was on top of him he struck him in the stomach with a tremendous punch. The tanker groaned. Two more direct, one to the face and the other to one side, were about to finish with their rival. The fight had to be decided. Alf had his opponent cornered, and Bert was about to bring his opponent down decisively.

"Damn braggart! The tanker roared, rebuilding himself, ready to continue.

But his final rush ended in the most resounding failure. Rudi had waited for him attentive to his slightest movements and when he lunged at him, he dodged slightly to the side and linking one leg with his right calf brought him to the ground with a tremendous blow. He was about to jump on him to complete his victory when Katia, who was contemplating the scene in terror, shouted:

"Watch out! A surveillance patrol is coming!

The tanker stood up semi-conscious, and everyone stopped the fight paying attention. Hurried footsteps sounded outside. The door slammed open and a squad of surveillance stormed the premises. The corporal stared at the wreckage with a frown. His soldiers had already separated the contenders and were putting some order in the battered local.

"Beautiful! "He exclaimed, furious." And do you call this rest? You all deserve to go to a punishment squad! "He pointed to the tankers." To your accommodation! And as for you, "he added, addressing the grenadiers," go to the barracks before the lieutenant finds out what has just happened.

Rudi had a tremendous scratch on his face. Katia approached solicitously with a clean towel that she dipped in a little "vodka" and applied to the wound.

"Does it hurt a lot? He asked tenderly.

"Oh! This is nothing ", Rudi boasted, and taking advantage of the confusion that still reigned in the place, he added under his breath." When could you and I talk for a while alone ...? How about an hour from now, by the bridge?

The girl looked flustered left and right and after a moment's hesitation answered:

"Good. I'll see if I can slip away.

CHAPTER III

The day had dawned bright and radiant. A true spring day, even though winter was close at hand. Early in the morning, the patrol lined up in front of the barracks with full weapons. The "feldwebel" reviewed. In a few moments, the lieutenant appeared, smiling and dynamic, completely recovered from the fatigue of the last days.

"Boys" once said all firm and in silicon. Headquarters has seen fit to congratulate us on our latest raid. I am pleased to inform you and hope that this patrol will never be unworthy of the fame it has so deservedly earned. Now we will go to the field to exercise, since as you all know, we must always keep fit and ready for action. If you behave well, you can have the afternoon at your leisure.

A short order and the patrol set off. They crossed the bridge where Rudi and Katia had met for the first time the night before. The grenadier looked slightly dreamy.

"That woman has him upset," Bert commented.

"We have never seen him like this" added Alf. Are you losing faculties?

Arrived at the outskirts of the town, the lieutenant chose a rugged terrain and partly covered by towering grass.

First of all, "he said", we will carry out a simulation of hand-to-hand fighting ... It seems to me that you have somewhat forgotten, and it does not hurt that we exercise a little this important part of our task.

A general laugh broke out in the ranks.

"What the hell is wrong with them? Asked the 'feldwebel', turning to the officer.

"I don't know", the lieutenant replied with an enigmatic smile. But, of course, they are going to know what is good. Well "he continued, hiding his amusement a little." You are going to divide into two sides and you will attack each other viciously, like true savages. You understood me? Do not see anyone waver or play "soft." Think that the person in front of you is the enemy himself, and shake him with all your might.

The two sides were formed instantly. One of them was commanded by the feldwebel, the other by the corporal. The latter consisted of Bert, Rudi and Alf. They stripped off their tunics and their athletic torsos gleamed in the sun. Rudi exercised his muscles, revealing biceps capable of competing with those of the toughest and most seasoned professional boxer.

At a signal, the two sides parted, lined up facing each other, ready to charge. Rudi threatened his rivals and called them "petty" and "scrawny." However, the group commanded by the "feldwebel" Engerling looked magnificent with their sunburned grenadiers ready to shake these braggarts boldly.

The lieutenant stood on an eminence on the ground and said:

"Stay tuned for the whistle. One touch means to attack. Two, stop the fight. And remember that you will act as if you really were facing the enemy. You must beat each other mercilessly. It doesn't matter if you hurt each other. They'll heal you later in the medicine cabinet.

He raised the whistle to his lips. One long touch, and they all plunged into the fray, roaring and "hooray!" The corporal grabbed the first opponent by the waist and the two rolled on the grass, striking each other with real fury. Alf, Bert, and Rudi did not linger in pondering methods or planning their attack. The enemy was upon them and it was necessary to show that it was not for nothing that they were called in the regiment "the inseparable three." They formed a stone wall with their bodies and their three opponents crashed into it, without being able to knock it down in any way. It was useless for them to put into practice the various fighting systems learned in the course of the long struggle. Rudi, Alf, and Bert remained at their posts and within minutes the initiative had passed into their hands. Taking advantage of a moment of confusion, Rudi grabbed two of his rivals by the neck and with a strong jerk caused their heads to collide violently. The two grenadiers fell to the ground in bruises. Bert and Alf took advantage of that brief moment of respite to wipe their sweaty foreheads with their handkerchief. The third opponent was about to go on the offensive when two whistle blasts sounded clearly in the calm morning air.

"A quarter of an hour break" announced the lieutenant. Then we will continue.

The grenadiers sat on the grass, Rudi took out a cigarette and started to light it.

"Didn't you see something strange in all this? "He asked his two companions." What will come of this eagerness to make us literally tear ourselves apart? Did a snitch tell you about yesterday and want to teach us a lesson?

"Hey ... well it's true, we've never seen him so vicious" muttered Bert thoughtfully.

Alf touched Rudi with his elbow, pointing him in the direction of a path that ran a short distance away. A female figure was watching them intently. Rudi jumped. It was Katia coming back from washing her clothes in the river.

"Listen to me for a moment" he told them. Make sure they don't see me. I'm going to chat with her for a few minutes.

"I wouldn't do that foolishness in your place," Bert advised him. As the lieutenant sees you, he is going to give you a package that you will remember for a long time. You know how it is in these discipline things.

"Bah! I do not mind. Besides, if I take it, I will be alone. I'll be back shortly. Just a couple of words. Meanwhile, if they ask about me, hide as best you can. Agree?

"Okay," Bert grumbled. But be careful and don't linger too long ... although I admit that Katia is capable of upsetting anyone's brain.

"The poor man is caramelized like a schoolboy" Alf commented, with an expression of pity.

Rudi clapped them on the shoulder and walked away, crouching through the grasses, just as the lieutenant looked away. The young woman was startled when she saw him emerge before her from the bushes. Rudi didn't beat around the bush. He took her by the hands and drawing her towards him asked her:

"Will we meet tonight... at yesterday's site? Right? If you tell me no, I am capable of crossing before the grenadiers when they shoot at the target.

She was staring at him ecstatically. He patted the muscles in his arm, letting out an admiring expression.

"Strong, huh? "Rudi boasted." Well, look "and he stuck out his chest, bulging it until it looked like it was going to explode.

"Does your wound hurt? "Katia asked, gently caressing the place on her cheek, where she now wore a white plaster band.

"What wound? Rudi said, pretending to be oblivious. A hiss was heard at that precise moment.

"It is Bert who warns me. I have to go. Well, Katia, until the evening. Truth?

"Until the night.

And Rudi walked away with the same precautions with which he had approached. At the precise moment that he was standing next to his companions, the lieutenant ordered:

"Ready to continue the exercise...! But I notice you a little tired, especially Rudi, Bert and Alf.

"Are we tired? "Said Rudi." You do not know us, my lieutenant ...

"It seems to me that I know you too well. Well, place the targets and we are going to carry out marksmanship exercises with the submachine guns.

The order was carried out and soon a series of gusts resounded, shaking the calm atmosphere of the morning.

CHAPTER IV

Major Braun, commander of the 3rd Battalion, under whose direct orders the patrol was, had his accommodation in an "isba" located just a short distance from the road. A sentry armed with a submachine gun and several hand bombs secured to his belt stood guard at the door.

Seeing Lieutenant Wahrenfels approaching, the sentry squared stiffly, clearing his way. An orderly came quickly.

"The major awaits you, my lieutenant. Over here, please.

The lieutenant entered the compound of the "isba", divided into two sections by a curtain that crossed it from part to part. In the first one you could see the major's field bed and a few toiletries. In the most reserved he had his operational maps and plans, placed on a wide table.

Lieutenant Wahrenfels respectfully waited for his boss to invite him in, which the major did by half-opening the curtain and saying:

"Go ahead Lieutenant. We need to talk.

Major Braun was a man of superior stature, strong and healthy. He was in his forties and there was a certain stamp of distinction on his whole person, as well as an unusual energy and dynamism. He motioned for the lieutenant to sit down and handed him a pack of cigarettes.

"You smoke" he said. The matter what has compelled me to call you is of the utmost importance. It's about nothing less than ensuring our superiority in the sector. As you may already know, the first and second sections of the fourth company occupy a ledge in front of Novo Skolki. From the ledge in question we dominate the Kolpino-Leningrad highway, making it difficult or even impossible to travel along it. Now, the enemy, who undoubtedly wants to increase his traffic, judging by some symptoms observed these days ... and that smell quite bad to me, has just assembled a battery of heavy mortars that has harassed us without rest since yesterday ... But, better It will be that we observe this plan "and he handed the lieutenant one in which the enemy and his own positions were marked with different colors. He watched the lieutenant,

"All right, my commander" Wahrenfels said, knowing in advance what that preamble was going to lead to. " And you want ...

"Get rid of those mortars" concluded the major, briefly, adding after a brief pause: I don't think things will be difficult for your boys ... it's what they call a "little excursion to graze." But act with caution and without making too much of a fuss. They will approach with the utmost silence. They will take out the sentries and battery servants and place delayed blast charges. Then retreat at maximum speed, returning from exactly the same place where you started ... that is, the ledge. Our artillery will remain alert in case it is necessary to protect them with a containment barrier. In a pinch, launch a green rocket, with a delayed fall. Try to be smart, and that no one is left behind. If you can bring a prisoner or two, please do so. They will always serve to provide some data.

Major Braun got up. He took a few steps across the room sucking on his cigarette and added as the lieutenant got up, preparing to leave:

"You don't know how sorry I am to have interrupted your rest so abruptly. But in the present case, I need a patrol to finish the matter in a few minutes, without raising any alarm in the sector ... Good luck, Lieutenant "he said extending a hand that the lieutenant shook vigorously." And when he returns, he may have a surprise for the boys.

The lieutenant saluted and left. As he made his way to the barracks, he mentally reviewed the instructions he had received, trying not to forget any details. When he passed the door of the compound, the grenadiers rose, standing at attention. Rudi, Alf and Bert looked at each other, making a mocking face. They knew exactly what it was about, before their boss opened his mouth.

"Boys" began the lieutenant. I just came from meeting Major Braun ... And I'm sorry to tell you that the break is over ... at least for today. We have "little grazing excursion" for tonight. At seven o'clock we will form with complete equipment at the entrance of the accommodation. "Feldwebel" Engerling, take care of ammunition and proceed to a general review. Let the boys clean and grease their weapons... and let no one forget the machete.

With that said, the lieutenant withdrew, reaching for the brim of his cap.

"Dammit! Rudi growled. What the hell is there to do now? And I had such an urgent matter ...!

He put on his hat, hurriedly fastened his belt, and added:

"I come soon!

"Hey! Where are you going? Bert asked, getting up.

"If they ask about me, say I'll be gone for a few minutes, just to ...

"I, in your place" Alf interrupted him ", I would hurry. You already know that the lieutenant does not admit jokes when it is necessary to act.

"Don't worry," said Rudi. You won't even notice.

And with that said, he disappeared.

* * *

Katia came and went between the tables, serving the first customers of the afternoon. But although apparently absorbed in her task, her thoughts flew far away towards the manly figure of Rudi, whom she imagined at that moment, lying on his bunk ... thinking about her as well. But perhaps it would be better to end this useless adventure. The fate of a soldier is so uncertain...! And when Rudi left, they would most likely never meet again.

A shadow blocked the door. Katia looked up. Rudi was watching her from the doorway. The young woman smiled at him and he made a brief sign, inviting her out.

"Katia" said the grenadier, once they were somewhat far from the "isba" ". Tonight ... I have to go out. We will leave in a little while. But first I would like to ask you one thing ... "He hesitated. She looked at him deeply moved. " I would like your promise that if some damn tanker "grit his teeth" makes love to you, remember me and reject him.

"Promised, Rudi" she replied, looking at his face. You won't be away for long, will you?

"I do not believe it. And when I return ...

They held hands.

"Goodbye, Katia. Or rather, goodbye ... "Auf wieder sehen."

"" Dosvidania, Rudi. " And be very careful.

"Don't worry sweetie. The Wahrenfels Patrol is the lucky patrol. I have never been able to get sent to the hospital to rest for a little while... I miss it!

* * *

Alf and Bert greeted their comrade with recriminations and sarcasm.

"The 'feldwebel' asked for you, and we had to tell him that you had gone for a drink," said the first.

"Well, who tells you I haven't? I was in the tavern. And why go to a tavern if not to drink?

"Stop ironies. How about your Russian? Have you cried a lot?

"Not. As the absence will last a short time ...

"As long as some tanker doesn't conquer it.

"There are no tankers for Rudi.

Well, guys. Less talk "intervened the" feldwebel "". And you Rudi, try not to disappear without warning, like recently. I don't feel like having complications with the boss.

At seven o'clock the patrol lined up in front of their accommodation with the complete equipment. Lieutenant Wahrenfels appeared with rigorous punctuality. His inspection was brief. There was the hum of an engine, and soon a truck pulled up in front of the grenadiers.

"Up! Ordered the lieutenant.

They accommodated themselves in the best possible way, and in a few minutes the truck was moving towards the front, from which came reddish flashes accompanied by the hoarse boom of artillery shells and the distant clatter of machine guns.

CHAPTER V

When they reached about four kilometers from the front lines, the vehicle's safety lights went off and the vehicle continued in complete darkness to the battalion command post. The lieutenant descended to inform his superior, who had already been warned in advance, by the colonel of the regiment. The exchange of views was very brief.

"We will stand by in case it is necessary to help them," Major Baer said. In a pinch don't forget to launch the green rocket. The phone is ready and the cannons aimed at that happy fortified battery.

"At your orders, my commander... And until we return.

"Bye. Good luck, "replied Major Baer, saluting.

Lieutenant Wahrenfels called his men. Once gathered around him, he proceeded to inform them of the most important details of the operation.

"In short," he declared, "we can call this incursion" silent and effective. " Our primary goal is to eliminate sentries and crew without causing unnecessary fuss. Once the "loudspeakers" are removed, we will proceed to place dynamite charges in the appropriate places. The withdrawal will be done in the same way. If there is danger or the enemy raises the alarm, Schmit will launch a green rocket ... and watch out for color confusion, eh, boy? Don't go throw a broadside in the ribs.

A link was in charge of leading them to the ledge.

"It's going to be child's play," said the corporal, as the group set off. I bet anything we found them sleeping.

"I wouldn't brag too much in your place," said Bert. Do you remember that time when ...?

"Silence! "Ordered the lieutenant." Enough of the comments! As soon as I hear one speak, I am going to send him twenty meters to the forefront. 'Feldwebel', please circulate the password: 'Flakbatterie'.

The grenadiers advanced, trying not to make noise with their footsteps. Upon reaching the outposts protected by sandbags, they prepared their weapons and checked the hand bombs that were distributed along the belt. At a signal from the lieutenant they advanced toward the wire. The link indicated the existing passage in itself, and the lieutenant took good note of it so as not to get lost when they returned. The night was gloomy. Rudi secured the magazine of his "submachine gun."

Once in "no man's land" precautions redoubled. They advanced crouched. The lieutenant oriented himself with his luminous pocket compass. It was necessary to approach without the enemy suspecting anything. The battery was about two hundred meters ahead, a little to the left. A luminous rocket rose into the air and the grenadiers threw themselves to the ground as one man. A machine gun fired a burst above their heads. They dragged on. It was necessary to cross the enemy trench, since the battery was a little further back, and then back off without making the slightest noise. The success or failure of the company depended on it.

At a signal from the lieutenant, the grenadiers stretched out on the ground, perfectly still.

"Send a scout," whispered Wahrenfels to the "feldwebel."

The latter tapped the nearest grenadier on the arm, who crawled toward the trench. The minutes passed slowly, turning the brief wait into an eternity. The explorer returned in a short time.

"A sentry stands guard in the trench" he said.

"We must eliminate it" was the blunt order of Lieutenant Wahrenfels.

"Rudi and Bert" murmured the 'feldwebel'. And have Alf cover them.

The two comrades winked at each other and crawled away, while Alf slid behind him with the "submachine gun" at the ready. In a few minutes they were back.

"He fell like a chick," Bert reported.

The others smiled at each other.

"Now we can't entertain ourselves," said the lieutenant. As they discover that sentinel eliminated, I do not give a cigarette for our skin.

They cut the wire with special pliers, fitted with insulating handles in anticipation of possible electrical cables, and then they crossed one after another, jumping over the suppressed sentry. The fortification could be seen from about two hundred meters away, perfectly visible because of the disturbed earth. Most likely a man or two had stationed there, while the rest slept in some nearby shack.

The lieutenant raised his right hand and the patrol split into two groups, one under his command and the other under the feldwebel. The latter included Rudi, Bert, Alf and the corporal. The first would eliminate the guards and proceed to the placement of explosive charges. The second was aimed at destroying the mortar crew and taking a prisoner or two, according to the instructions received. The brigade made a gesture and the group moved, while the lieutenant's moved away in the opposite direction. They took a little detour. After having traveled a hundred meters, they made out a mound, indicating that under it was the shelter. Rudi jerked his thumb at himself and the feldwebel nodded.

They crawled forward. The silence was absolute. Only the occasional isolated shot fired from time to time. The two groups converged, one on the position and the other on the shack located a very short distance from it. As the feldwebel and his men studied the terrain, two thumps were heard. The lieutenant's had just finished off the guardians of the pieces. Rudi walked only to the door and opened it carefully, pushing with the barrel of his "submachine gun." Inside, the atmosphere was unbreathable. Five Russians slept soundly, snoring. Rudi shook the first of them, while ordering him in his language:

"Get up, boy! To relieve!

The soldier got to his feet, grunting, and without turning on any lights, he strapped on his holster and picked up his rifle. Standing on either side of the door, Bert and Alf waited for him with their little hand hoes. There was a knock and the Russian slumped to the ground. The remaining four were coming out at intervals, awakened by Rudi, to receive an accurate blow to their hard teeth, with withering and decisive effects, which was knocking them down one after another. The operation was carried out successfully, in the midst of the most complete silence. Four Russians were lying on the ground when Rudi came out pushing the fifth soldier with the barrel of his 'submachine gun'.

"There's no more? Asked the 'feldwebel'.

"There's nothing left in there but bedbugs," Rudi replied, scratching himself vigorously and breathing in the cool night air at the top of his lungs. " What a smell! Again I will not forget a good insecticide. And he made a gesture of fumigating with the barrel of his pistol.

For his part, the lieutenant and his boys had already completed the placement of the explosives. The task could be considered finished. All that remained was to withdraw in good order with the prisoner, without raising any alarm. The trench and wire were crossed. They had traveled a hundred meters when rumors sounded behind them. The lieutenant ordered to hurry. A machine gun had begun to rattle. A rocket went up into the air. One hundred more meters. Suddenly, a horrible explosion shook the ground. The mortar battery had been destroyed. Rudi smiled.

"To the race! Ordered the lieutenant.

Disregarding all precautions, the grenadiers crossed at full speed the distance that separated them from their own trenches. Now there were already several machines that spewed fire on them.

"Did I launch the rocket? Asked the grenadier in charge of them.

"No need" replied the lieutenant. We would uselessly discover our position and, on the other hand, it seems to me that ours have already begun to act.

Indeed, intermittent glows shone on the horizon. In a few seconds the artillery shells crossed over their heads with impressive whistles and a real hell was unleashed behind them. They were at the barbed wire. The lieutenant got his bearings. The pass was near. They gave the password and in a few seconds they were all jumping into the trench.

A brief inspection and the lieutenant ordered:

"To home!

"Home Sweet Home! "Sighed Rudi." What is my Russian doing? "He added, pulling out his pipe and filling it with tobacco as the group set off from the trench.

"How comfortable I'm going to sleep! Bert muttered, with a tremendous yawn.

CHAPTER VI

The following morning, Lieutenant Wahrenfels had his grenadiers trained to inform them that by command order they would enjoy a week of absolute rest.

"Major Braun just told me" he informed them. This is the surprise I had in store for you. They are satisfied with our performance, which cannot but make me proud. We will only do theoretical exercises for a couple of hours a day and the rest of the time is yours... I trust it won't be too long. And now, break ranks and have fun out there!

The grenadiers were jubilant, Rudi, Alf and Bert slapped each other hard, laughing.

"The luckiest is Rudi" said Alf. At least he has a girlfriend to hang out with.

"Can't we have it? Asked Bert. Has this stunned man believed that only he conquers them? From now on I'm going to show you that they also melt for me.

"Shut up, you piece of tuna! Where are you going with that face?

"Have you believed that you are some Adonis?

"I am Apollo in person" Rudi boasted, puffing out his chest and twisting his cap.

When they got to the vicinity of the tavern, they saw Katia coming out with a basket of dirty clothes. Rudi hissed and the girl turned her head. An expression of deep joy was painted on her face.

"Where are you going, precious? Asked Rudi.

"Well, to the river to wash.

"Can I accompany you?

"Not. You better go in for a drink. I think it will suit you perfectly.

"If you don't serve it, you are going to look like poison to me.

"My father will serve it for you. I'll be right back.

"Come on, Rudi. Go with her "said Alf." Why so much dissimulation?

"I don't feel like going for a walk," replied the aforementioned. Let's have a drink.

The three entered the premises. Old Ivan was tending to the soldiers.

"'Vodka', 'vodka' and 'vodka'" asked Bert, pointing to himself and the others.

The old man nodded. Shortly after, he came with glasses and a bottle of liquor. Rudi served his two friends. He tried to appear carefree, but his thoughts were fixed on Katia, who at that moment would be by the river, in a certain beautiful place covered by tall grass and caressed by the breeze. Half an hour passed. The place was getting lively and most of the tables were already taken. The smoke invaded everything. Suddenly Rudi got up.

"I'm going to take a walk out there" he said. I want to breathe some fresh air.

"Fresh air? "Repeated Bert and Alf, looking at each other with a sly smile." Come on, go. And the longer it takes, the better... for you.

Rudi went out into the street. The sun was shining in the sky. Groups of soldiers came and went chatting and laughing. The war seemed very far away under that splendid sky, in that quiet and peaceful village. Rudi took the river path. Leaving the last houses behind, he descended the bank and then continued upstream. A thick vegetation grew lush in those places. He still walked quite a long way. Suddenly he saw her, crouched by the water in a small pool. He whistled from afar so as not to scare her. Seeing him, she got up and went out to meet him.

They held hands.

"How are you, Rudi? Nothing happened to you?

"You see that I am whole", he answered, moving a little so that she could contemplate him at her pleasure.

"Yes, yes" his blue eyes were shining with joy. I've thought about you a lot. And you? Did you remember poor Katia?

"What if I have remembered? I was thinking of nothing else but seeing you again as soon as possible ... here, by the river ... the two of us.

"No, Rudi. What is the use of feeding vain illusions? You will leave one day, never to return ... and I will stay here, with only your memory.

Rudi squeezed her hands tightly. They were in a quiet and secluded place, the sun already setting gilded the sky and a faint and aromatic breeze blew. He tried to pull her close, and she resisted. He had taken her by the arms. I wanted to kiss her. He felt the soft perfume of the young woman invade his senses. Katia jerked away and took a few steps away.

"No, Rudi, no" he said. It would be useless. Go with your friends. We'll see you later.

Rudi walked away to the road, grumpy. He waited for her by the bridge. In a little while he saw her coming with her basket of clothes. He grabbed a handle and the two of them headed toward the tavern. He let her go in alone and soon after he did.

Alf and Bert had dispensed most of the bottle. There was a barely contained euphoria in them.

"How did it go, boy? Bert asked, winking.

"It seems that he brings the face of few friends" Alf commented, for his part.

"Have you fought?

"Shut up, you idiots! "Exclaimed Rudi, unloading a punch on the table." And you, old man, bring another bottle.

They continued drinking. A Russian girl had begun to sing a melancholic song of the country and the three of them kept the beat with their heads. Katia stayed inside the house, avoiding going out. Bert and Alf were a bit dizzy. Rudi slowly emptied the bottle without apparently having any effect on the liquor. He was used to drinking and boasted of his stamina. However, on that occasion he would have preferred that the extremely strong liquor disturb his head as soon as possible, until he made him forget that Katia had not wanted to let him hold her in his arms.

It was late at night when the three of them left the premises. They walked arm in arm, with a somewhat unsure step, singing loudly. A patrol passed him.

"They are the" inseparable three "" commented a soldier.

"Too boastful" added another. Sure! How they are so spoiled! Those grenadiers think ...

"Would you do what they do? "The corporal interrupted him." You better shut up, you fool!

Alf, Bert, and Rudi were walking down the street. When they reached the barracks they redoubled their shouts, forcing the sentry to order them to be quiet. They entered the premises in an uproar. The "feldwebel" ordered them to report.

"Is that the example you know how to set? He "grunted." Luckily we're on rest and I don't want to bother you, otherwise ...

Rudi pulled the hat up to his eyes.

Hey, feldwebel! "Told him". Has a young woman never given you pumpkins?

The "feldwebel" was red with indignation. Two grenadiers got up and, taking the three comrades by the arm, forced them to sit on their beds. Rudi lay down on his. For a long time, the figure of Katia was circling through his brain assuming strange shapes. As soon as he saw her approaching him, affectionate and solicitous, her red lips parted in a smile, as if she was walking away, sullen and hostile, among the towering grass of the river bank. He slept very badly and had nightmares. He dreamed that he and Katia were holding hands through an enchanting place. Suddenly, the sky was covered with threatening clouds, lightning flashed and in its livid light, a horrible black individual, with a white skull on his forehead, attacked them and tried to take Katia away. Rudi struggled on his bunk,

Alf and Bert were snoring a little further. Rudi stayed awake for a long time. Outside, the sound of vehicles circulating on the road sounded, and far away, a muffled noise indicated the presence of the front. He made efforts to sleep. A thousand images crisscrossed his brain. Towards dawn a heavy slumber overcame him and soon he fell asleep in a deep and uneasy sleep.

CHAPTER VII

A tremendous jolt woke him up. Loud explosions shook the building. Window panes were shattering. The grenadiers had risen from their bunks and were trying to protect themselves as best they could against the thick walls. Dense smoke invaded everything. The explosions followed one another without interruption, turning the quiet village into a hell of flames and screams.

Alf, Bert and Rudi ran in the direction of a trench made a short distance from the house, as a refuge. The iron tempest raged on with chilling howls and horrible detonations that shook the ground.

"It's the 'twenty-one," said Bert. But how is it possible if until recently there were only medium-caliber artillery in the sector?

"They will have transported them these days" said Alf, impassive.

"This indicates that the train is again running behind the Russian lines. But hadn't our aviation destroyed the track? Asked Rudi.

"Aviation always thinks it destroys everything," said Bert. But it flies too high. There is no way to stick to the ground and place a good load of explosives in the right place.

The roar of the shocks continued. The villagers ran in terror in all directions. Some "isbas" were beginning to burn.

"As something happens to Katia ...! Rudi threatened, gnashing his teeth.

A girl had stopped a short distance from the trench where the three grenadiers had taken refuge. She was crying uncontrollably and looking in all directions looking for someone who could protect her. A projectile exploded so close to the creature that its clothes shuddered from the displacement of the air. Rudi put both hands on the edge of the trench, ready to come to his aid.

"Where are you going, fool? Asked Bert in alarm.

"In search of that girl... And then, to see my Katia.

He jumped out of the shelter and ran toward the girl. He caught her off balance and led her to his two comrades.

"Keep it there with you" he told them.

And he left again, undaunted by the smoke and shrapnel. Their own artillery was preparing to answer. The gleaming mouths of the batteries slowly rose to the proper angle. The servants with the openwork helmets positioned themselves strategically around the pieces. The grenades were swiftly circulated. The strikers were arranged. There were thirty heavy-caliber guns in the sector, in addition to some long-range mortars whose projectiles opened tremendous funnels and were capable of bringing down the most solid buildings and fortifications with a single blow. At a signal all the pieces vomited their load. There was a horrible hiss in the air and within seconds the projectiles were slamming down like destructive monsters on the opposing artillery positions.

Alf and Bert remained in their shelter with the abandoned girl. Some ambulances were going to town. The enemy artillery was spacing their shots and after half an hour the fire had completely ceased. Several houses were burning and the inhabitants of Novo-Skolki were preparing to fight the fires. Alf and Bert left the shelter ready to take part in the rescue tasks, like all the soldiers on leave. The bombardment had caused a good number of casualties among the civilian population. The heartbreaking scenes followed, and stretchers passed with corpses covered with blankets. Tremendous funnels opened in the streets and a thick mist and the smell of gunpowder and trilite still hung in the air.

At his command post, Major Braun was on the phone with the colonel of the regiment.

"My colonel, we have just suffered a tremendous bombardment by the opposing artillery. These are heavy-caliber guns that until now had not shown any signs of life in this sector. They have undoubtedly just been transported and emplaced. There is no doubt that the train is again running behind the Russian lines.

"Good, Commander", replied the colonel. We will pass the report on to the Division. In the meantime, build some shelters for the soldiers and the civilian population.

"At your orders, my colonel" and Major Braun hung up the receiver, proceeding immediately to give the pertinent instructions for the fulfillment of the order received.

* * *

Rudi had run like a madman, ignoring the explosions that were happening around him, shaking the ground as if an earthquake were taking place. One of them threw him against the wall of a burning "isba" and a thick log fell in flames a few inches from his head. Rudi continued his career in the direction of the tavern. Its interior was invaded by thick smoke from a nearby fire. There was no one around. Five projectiles tumbled into the street with a frightful roar. Rudi went outside. Katia must have been sheltering in the vicinity. He left the road and went out into the field. In the ravines you could see a good number of people huddled with their faces against the ground. He went a long way inspecting everything. Finally, next to an eminence of the land, he saw Katia. She was lying on the ground trying to protect herself in the best possible way. He jumped to her side. The young woman gave a cry of surprise.

"How are you, Katia? "He said". Has nothing happened to you?

"Nothing apart from the ghastly fear I'm going through.

It was shaking like a leaf. Rudi moved closer to her and put an arm around her waist, pulling her against him. The minutes passed slowly. But for the two lovers the bombing had ceased to exist. They lived in a dream world that had nothing to do with projectiles exploding a short distance away, screams of terror, smoke from explosions, and the collapse of modest homes.

* * *

Alf and Bert helped an elderly woman out of the rubble and then placed her on a stretcher. She suffered severe burns and two soldiers rushed her to the emergency kit. Some ambulances were already leaving for the nearest blood hospital.

"Where has Rudi been? Asked Alf stopping a bit to look in all directions.

"He'll be in some shelter," said Bert ironically, making an undulating gesture with his hands.

"I never would have thought a woman would make him so mocha!

"Hey look! Here it comes!

Indeed, Rudi was running. As soon as the bombardment stopped, his sense of duty prevailed, and after kissing Katia goodbye, he ran into town ready to help rescue.

The three comrades prepared for action. Some houses had to be propped up and others that threatened to collapse. The work was rough and tiring. By noon the smoke from the explosions had completely eclipsed, a radiant sun was shining, and huge funnels with charred edges and logs burning on the ground were left on the ground as traces of the tremendous bombardment. The population had suffered a good number of casualties and several soldiers were wounded, although not seriously.

Bert, Rudi, and Alf retired to their quarters with blackened faces and ripped uniforms. Shortly after, Lieutenant Wahrenfels came to inspect his troop. Other than some burns and bruises, the grenadiers had not suffered any serious damage.

"That trench must be deepened and covered with logs and earth," he told them. That way you will do a little exercise, to keep in shape, lest your muscles atrophy.

During the night, the German artillery continued firing intermittently on the enemy positions. There was a certain distressing feeling in the air, as if important events were approaching. A Russian plane, with the lights off, flew over the road, dropping some bombs on neighboring towns. The antiaircraft machine guns, stationed in the surroundings, responded by firing trails of tracer bullets into the air. Vigilance was ordered to be reinforced, and some motorcyclists circulated between the battalion command post and the town where the Division General Headquarters was located.

CHAPTER VIII

Two days passed. The town was recovering from the damage caused by the bombing. Life resumed its normal rhythm and as traces of the disaster were some ruins blackened by smoke and the tremendous gaps opened by the explosion of the projectiles. The soldiers on leave were circulating happily through the streets and in old Ivan's tavern it was difficult to find an available table.

Judging by certain symptoms, the command was proceeding to reinforce that sector. A company of sappers had come in and, after a short stay in Novo-Litka, set out for the front with their work supplies. The antiaircraft batteries located in strategic places remained alert. A battalion of tanks stationed in Krasnovardeisk detached some armored vehicles to the surrounding towns. Apparently, the enemy was trying some action to improve their positions before the winter with its snows and ice made all movement impossible.

The city of Leningrad, girded by the iron noose of German divisions, was trying to breathe. Only a railway linked it to the outside through the gap in Lake Ladoga, located to the north, towards the Finnish border, and by that single communication route the populous city received the necessary aid. Maintaining such a link with the outside was a vitally important objective for the besieged. The German aircraft dropped their bombs relentlessly on the railroad, but the imprecision of the air strikes was compounded by the speed with which the battalions of workers repaired the damage. Traffic, though precarious, continued. And proof of this was the recent bombardment of some towns, carried out with large caliber pieces recently transported to the front.

The High Command was studying a plan aimed at the definitive destruction of the railway. Once that was eliminated, the city could not sustain itself for more than a few months.

Meanwhile, the units continued their daily task, waiting for the moment to launch the attack. An observation post had been set up at Novo-Litka, with captive balloons, their silvery surfaces gleaming in the sun.

Alf, Bert and Rudi left their accommodation in the middle of the afternoon. The atmosphere was soft and calm. Mechanically they headed, their steps towards the tavern, Katia smiled at Rudi and greeted him with a cheerful gesture. They sat down to drink glasses of "vodka." As the young woman approached, Rudi said in a low voice:

"Why don't we go out for a walk? Do you want me to wait for you outside, darling?

"Eto nevozmoino"She answered in Russian But later veroyatno. I'll let you know.

Alf and Bert were looking at her without understanding the jargon.

"What are you proposing? "Asked the first." Something we can't know?

"Nothing in particular, guys. Just a little walk around the neighborhood. Is there something wrong with it?

"You have enough flies for us already, Rudi. So much walk up and down comes to scale anyone. Is it that you intend to let yourself be trapped by that young woman?

"Katia is wonderful" said Rudi rolling his eyes and letting out a deep sigh.

"And so naive! "Bert ironized." Watch her flirt with those drivers.

Indeed. Katia laughed at the joke of two transport soldiers who had left their trucks outside, on their way back from the front line. Rudi scowled at her. His eyes fired sparks.

"'There is no doubt" said Alf. The boy is jealous. Ha! Ha! Ha!

"Do not! "Bert cut him comically alarmed." Don't provoke him. I don't want the lieutenant to order us to hit each other like the other day.

Rudi got up and headed for the door. As he passed Katia, he said in Russian with an irritated accent:

"I'll wait for you next to the last house, near the bridge.

And he started walking trying to contain his nervousness.

Katia took a long time to come. He came with an easygoing and cheerful air. When she reached him, she took him by the arms and said, laughing:

"But what's the matter with you, my Rudi? Are you jealous? But, if those boys were the sea of friendly! One of them was explaining to me that ...

"I don't care what he was explaining to you.

He took her by the arm and they started off into the field. The evening shadows were beginning to invade everything. The sky, of a pure blue, was darkening and a star was shining in the height. Katia pressed herself against him.

"I'm cold" he said.

Rudi put an arm around her shoulders. He felt her warm body press against his. The smell of her hair intoxicated him. They stopped among some trees, near the stream. Katia sat on a mound and Rudi did the same next to her. They were holding hands, looking into each other's eyes.

"Katia" he began ", I ... I love you. I understand that it is foolish, but I can't help it. The other night, while we were performing, I was only thinking about you. And for the first time since I was in the war, I wanted to return safe and sound ... just to be by your side again ... and talk to you, like now.

"I love you too, Rudi. Fate has put us in front of each other. War is cruel, but one day it will end, and then maybe you and I can stay together forever ... But what is the use of having illusions? You will leave again and I will stay here thinking about your return. Perhaps you will return to your country and you will never remember Katia again.

Tears came to her eyes. Rudi drew her to him gently. She relented. Their lips met in a kiss.

"Whatever happens" he whispered "I will always love you. Will you come with me, eh, Katia? You will see how happy we will be when all this is over and peace reigns on earth again.

They remained in deep ecstasy for a long time. It was already dark at night. The stars were blazing above the sky. In the distance, a bugle sounded. The muffled sound of trucks traveling down the road reached them.

"We have to go," Katia muttered. My father will be uneasy.

Rudi got up and, holding out his hands, helped her up. They started back slowly, without waking up from their reverie. The grenadier accompanied her to the very door of the tavern. They kissed again in the dark.

"See you tomorrow, Katia ... And dream of me.

"See you tomorrow, Rudi.

Alf and Bert were already in the barracks, stretched out on their bunk beds when their comrade arrived.

"What hours, friend! How was the show? The first said.

Rudi grunted grumpily. I was not kidding. He stretched out on his mat and stood still, staring out into space.

"The allegation still lasts," Alf added. You have to see how low a man can fall!

He turned around and settled down to sleep. Bert regarded Rudi with a disdainful air and, picking up a newspaper, began to read by the dim light of a light bulb.

A distant rumor was perceived that little by little it was approaching. Several squadrons of planes crossed space. The grenadiers listened carefully.

"Where will those go? Asked one of them.

"I don't give a damn," answered Bert "as long as they don't download around here.

The rumor drifted away. Before long, almost imperceptible shaking shook the ground. The bombs exploded over the besieged city, while dozens of searchlights scoured the sky in search of the attacking devices and the anti-aircraft guns discharged their shrapnel in the air, in search of the steel wings that marked their path with a trail of death and destruction. Bert turned off the light, and after a while he was snoring peacefully as the planes buzzed on their way back outside.

CHAPTER IX

"To form! "Shouted the 'feldwebel'.

It was seven in the morning. The grenadiers rushed to take their place in the ranks. The lieutenant came to witness the list. One by one, they answered when they heard his name. It was a mere routine, which the lieutenant imposed so that he would not lose the habit of barracks discipline. Some services were appointed and the "feldwebel" was going to order breaking ranks, when the lieutenant stopped him with a gesture.

"Rudi, Bert and Alf will come to my accommodation" he said. I have an important matter to communicate to you.

"What the hell does he want? Rudi muttered.

"Maybe they've given us the first-class Iron Cross and a permit to Berlin," said Bert with a grimace.

The lieutenant was walking away and the three grenadiers followed him. The chief of the patrol stopped when he reached the door of his "isba."

"Come in, guys" he told them. We'll have a drink and chat.

"So much kindness scares me" Rudi said softly.

They sat down at the table and the lieutenant began without further ado:

"The situation has gotten slightly complicated these days. Apparently, the Russians have reinforcements that can only have come to them by means of the railroad that we have tried by all means to destroy, without being absolutely achieved to date. However, some unforeseeable circumstance may occur that helps improve your communications. Major Braun called me last night to inform me that it is necessary to find out something ... And for this there are only two systems: to make an excursion through enemy terrain, personally observing what happened, or to strike a hand against the trenches, bringing some prisoners to help us unravel the enigma. The Major and

I came to the conclusion that three determined grenadiers can do the latter without too much noise, and to the complete satisfaction of the Command. I immediately thought of you. Tell me honestly what you think. Of course, I am not going to force you and if any of you prefer to stay, let them say so clearly.

"Look at you, my lieutenant," Rudi replied. He knows that we love these little chores. How many Russians do you want? Is twenty enough for you? And I will say more: if you authorize me, I will go alone.

Two big hands fell on his shoulders, about to knock him to the ground. Alf and Bert threatened him with their fists.

"Good. Do not fight about it "said the lieutenant smiling." The three of you will go and I hope you are lucky she served you "vodka." "The operation seems simple, but the Command attributes extraordinary importance to it. The definitive planning of some of the operations under study depends on the statements of these prisoners, so be very careful, agile and cautious.

He unrolled a blueprint and proceeded to instruct them in the details of the coup. In general, it was a question of surprising isolated sentries along a trench that extended in front of the positions of the fourth company of the Second Battalion and bringing them without making any noise, or of surprising an entire squad asleep in their hut and force her to walk between the barrels of her "submachine guns" in the direction of her own lines.

"You will slide like cats, and unless you are sure of success, do not act. I'd rather come back safe and sound, empty-handed, than wounded or battered with a Russian or two. You will take light equipment and you will leave in the middle of the afternoon towards the front line positions. Captain Schmidt awaits you.

"What do you think? "Asked Bert as he left." This is our famous break?

"Well" said Alf. I was already getting bored. Besides, the thing promises to be fun, right, Rudi?

"Of course. On the other hand, it's just about missing one night. Something like when in other times one went to have a party with friends, not returning until dawn.

After lunch they went over their equipment. They carefully cleaned his "submachine gun," checked the edge of the machete, and stocked up on hand bombs.

"Are you planning to go see Katia? Bert asked Rudi.

"Yes, but I won't tell you anything about tonight's job. What do I get out of making the poor girl suffer?

At the quartermaster store they collected a light cold supply which they placed in the small side bag secured to the belt. It would be four thirty when a truck came to pick them up.

Captain Schmidt shook hands with them once they reached the front line.

"I already suspected it would be you" he said. Consequences of enjoying so much fame! Come to my shack and we'll have a glass of brandy.

Once inside the shelter, he briefly briefed them on the condition of the trench from which they would exit and through which they would seek to return.

An hour passed. It had gotten dark. The captain called a liaison. They shook hands.

"Good luck, guys" wished you. And until the return. Don't bring a whole company ... We wouldn't know where to put it.

The link led them to the outpost. The night movement had begun. Loose shots rang out and the occasional machine gun rattled, firing their tracer bullets. They crawled across the open path in the wire. The positions were very close and precautions had to be taken from the beginning. They continued to crawl like stalking beasts through no-man's-land. With their eyes fixed straight ahead, Rudi, Bert and Alf stopped from time to time holding their breath to hear better. The rockets rose into the air, diffusing their livid clarity for a few seconds, then went out with a click. They made a detour to line up the enemy trench on the side that, according to company information, was the most unguarded. When they arrived in front of the sandbags they stopped to study the terrain.

"We will advance in the following way" said Rudi in a low voice ": One from the bottom of the trench. This will be myself. The other two above, Alf on the right side and Bert on the left. Above all, do not let them scream or shoot, or launch an alarm rocket. If we catch them sleepy we can bring at least five or six.

They redoubled the precautions. Bert tripped over a tin can, cursed. They walked fifty meters with hardly any breath. The slightest oversight could cost them their lives. The trench towards a bend. On the other side a shadow stood out in confusion against the disturbed earth. Rudi made a sign. They glided like cats. Rudi was a few meters from the Russian. He heard something and turned his head.

"Kotori téper tchasse? He asked, not at all suspicious.

"Téper sefn" Rudi replied in a calm voice.

"Fear me loutchné.

He was undoubtedly awaiting his relief. The barrel of a "submachine gun" embedded itself in his ribs, while Rudi ordered him through clenched teeth:

"Hush or I'll dry you out!

The Russian's eyes widened in surprise. Two more "submachine guns" were pointed at him over the trench. It was useless to resist. He raised his arms and Rudi stripped him of his weapons.

"Take care of him, Alf. And be careful not to let him escape.

They were about to continue when footsteps sounded in the trench. Two men were approaching. Rudi, Alf, and Bert had stretched out on the ground forcing the prisoner to do the same. It was the relief trooper and a sergeant, no doubt inspecting the posts. Bert was about to whistle. Nothing less than a sergeant! After some sandbags, Rudi waited for the couple to come out onto the parapet. He signaled and three "submachine guns" lined up the Russians, one from above and two from both sides of the trench, since Bert had dropped to the bottom of the trench to prevent them from fleeing down the opposite side. The Russians did not resist. It was completely useless.

Withdrawal had to be undertaken, without causing any alarm. They went back the way they had come. The night was filled with rumors. An enemy patrol passed a short distance. They waited with tense nerves until he was gone. Bert briefly surveyed the surroundings. They came out of the trench. The return was tiring in the extreme from having to crawl along taking care of the prisoners. As soon as they had moved away a little, Rudi said in a low voice to his two comrades:

"Good hunting, huh? Major Braun is going to give us a happy hug!

"I have never seen an easier thing in my life," said Bert. It was like reaching into a burrow and pulling three rabbits by the ears.

"The good thing about it is that nobody is going to believe it," Alf added. The story will have to be dramatized a bit. In a few minutes they made out the barbed wire. The sentry stopped them and they answered the password. Captain Schmidt could not believe their eyes. They continued to the place where the truck was waiting and around midnight they appeared at the command post with the three prisoners. Major Braun's surprise was immense. Those boys were worth their weight in gold. I cordially shake your hand. Two soldiers armed with "machine guns" led the prisoners to the regimental command post, where they would be interrogated. Shortly after, Alf Bert and Rudi, stretched out on their mats ready to sleep peacefully until the new day dawned.

CHAPTER X

"I have asked the lieutenant for permission to go to Krasnovardeisk and he has given it to me," Rudi told his friends that morning, when the three of them were leaving the accommodation.

"Wow, man! Alf exclaimed. And ... are you going alone?

"Well ... I would have liked very much for you to come with me, but once there I will be quite busy and ...

"Good. Good. By the way, an hour ago I saw Katia get into a truck. Wouldn't he also go to Krasnovardeisk?

What the hell do I know? Do you think he keeps me up to date on everything he does?

They stationed themselves at the gasoline pump located at the exit of the town, where most of the trucks that circulated in that sector stopped. Soon a formidable "Henschel" with a trailer appeared. Rudi made a sign. The truck stopped to refuel.

"Where are you guys going? He asked the drivers.

"We will reach Krasnovardeisk and by mid-afternoon we will be back.

"Magnificent! I'm going with you.

He got into the vehicle. Other soldiers were already seated inside. He waved to his two friends as the truck started up.

"Goodbye!... And have fun! Alf yelled at him.

Rudi shook both hands in contemptuous mockery. It was not easy to fool his friends. The truck was bumping down the uneven road amid the monotonous hum of its powerful engine. Krasnovardeisk disappeared over the horizon after an hour. It was a huge and populous city, where German divisions had installed the services of the sector. Soldiers, whose gray uniforms were mixed with the rags of the civilian population, were always wandering its streets. The cafes were always lively and in some restaurants meals were served, although at prices only affordable for those who had plenty of money.

Katia was waiting for him, as arranged the night before, in the main square, in front of the Orthodox church, with its golden Byzantine domes. She was very pretty in her new dress and her headscarf, in the style of the country. She smiled at him showing her very white teeth and advanced towards him with her arms outstretched. They walked slowly, enjoying the spectacle of the city. They entered one or two stores and Rudi presented her with some trinkets, which she received amid exclamations of delight. Later they went to eat at a restaurant. Sitting at the white tablecloth, they gazed into each other's eyes. A waiter was solicitous. The menu was simple, but it was a real treat, considering the circumstances. Rudi allowed himself to order a bottle of wine, which they sipped slowly. Through the windowpanes the crowd could be seen coming and going in uninterrupted current. After eating they went to the park.

"Look at what a beautiful pond! Katia exclaimed.

They approached the water surrounded by greenery and contemplated each other in its clear reflection.

"Katia, do you know that you really look beautiful today?

The young woman's eyes sparkled with joy and she squeezed Rudi's arm, drawing even closer to him. They changed in silence for a long time.

"How I would like to stay here forever... with you! Rudi muttered. In a town like this, where at least you can live and where the presence of the front does not threaten every moment.

"Don't get your hopes up, Rudi, you and I can't even think of such things. Your destiny is to fight ... and mine to wait for you.

"Maybe some day...!

"Forget that we have to go back to Novo-Skolki. Let's forget that you are a soldier and I am a Russian girl. Let's take advantage of these moments and not remember tomorrow.

"Yes. Maybe it's for the best "muttered Rudi thoughtfully.

They stayed in the park until mid-afternoon. Suddenly Rudi looked at his watch. You had to hurry if you wanted to get back in the same truck. Katia would do it a little later, with the villagers she had come with and who were doing some shopping in the city. They kissed passionately.

"Goodbye, Katia. If you come back early, we'll still see each other for a bit tonight, right?

"I think so, Rudi. Wait for me by the bridge. I'll go even if it's just to give you another kiss.

Rudi waited at the agreed corner for the truck to pass. This one did not take long to appear.

"How have you been, grenadier? Asked one of the drivers.

"In the city you always have a good time", Rudi answered, climbing into the cabin. The downside is that they don't give you permission for more than one day ...

The truck started back. The flat, monotonous landscape slowly passed before Rudi's eyes, who stared blankly before him, seeing nothing. The kilometers passed one after another. The heavy-duty truck kept moving smoothly and smoothly.

"A cigarette? "Offered the driver.

Rudi agreed and proceeded to turn it on. The puffs of smoke filled the cabin little by little. Rudi lowered the window glass a few inches. Suddenly, his ears, pricked with constant alertness, heard a noise that stood out above the buzzing of the vehicle. The driver looked at him questioningly.

"Something wrong? "I ask.

Rudi finished lowering the glass and stuck his head out. There was no doubt about it. A tremendous bombardment was taking place a short distance away, perhaps in the direction of Novo-Skolki. As they ascended a small hill, the landscape expanded before their eyes. A thick cloud of smoke rose above the horizon, covering a considerable area of land. Unconsciously, the driver sped up. The explosions followed one another with tremendous roar. You could feel the ground shaking despite the distance. They advanced a few kilometers. When bending a curve they perceived the flames of the heavy caliber projectiles.

"They will not have left a house standing" said the driver. Let's wait a few minutes. I don't want to uselessly expose my car.

The bombardment went on for a few more minutes. Then the shots became more spaced, and at last it stopped. Dense cloud of smoke hung in space. The smell of gunpowder reached them. Many houses were burning. The vehicle advanced to the outskirts of town. The show was awesome. Very few houses remained unscathed, Rudi broke into a run. People fled in terror in all directions. Mangled corpses were seen lying in the street. An alarm siren let out its tragic moans. Rudi walked through the rubble toward the barracks. Alf and Bert met him. Their faces were blackened by smoke. All the components of the patrol were preparing to rescue how many people lay under the collapsed houses.

"The other day was nothing compared to this one" Bert told him, panting.

The three of them ran towards a place where lamentations and screams sounded. Smoking logs had to be cleared away, walls knocked down, living creatures and corpses removed from the ruins. Hardly any other house had been spared from the bombing. The barracks were seriously damaged.

"It seems to me that they are going to evacuate the town" said Alf. At least that's what I've heard the lieutenant say.

Katia's house was almost destroyed. Only a small part would be saved, the one where the premises destined for a tavern was located, and some of the home of its owners. Rad: felt his heart clench. Old Ivan was staring disconsolately at the ruin of his home. Rudi patted him on the back, trying to cheer him up.

The salvage went on until late at night. Katia and Rudi did not remember, more than their interview. The first had arrived two hours after the end of the bombardment. She wept inconsolably at the ruins and then dedicated herself to moving and healing the wounded with the other women. SI bombardment had also affected several neighboring towns. The road was filled with fugitives who were heading to the rear with the belongings they had been able to save from the catastrophe.

That night and when relative calm reigned over the town, the lieutenant gathered his men in front of the ruins of the barracks.

"Collect all your material" he told them. I have been urgently called to the command post. When I return, they must be ready for whatever the colonel orders.

And he left in a light car that was waiting for him a short distance away. The grenadiers busied themselves with ordering the material and cleaning it superficially. Fortunately, the weapons and ammunition had not been lost.

"I foresee events" murmured Rudi, looking abstractedly towards the place where the lieutenant had wandered off ... "And not good, by the way.

CHAPTER XI

"Come in," Colonel Weiss said, when the lieutenant had knocked on the door of his regimental commander's quarters.

Lieutenant Wahrenfels stood at attention, Colonel Weiss waved him, motioning him to sit down. He was a tall, stocky man, with almost cropped hair, who was impeccably dressed in a uniform in which a multitude of decorations stood out, some of them obtained in the First World War, when with the rank of lieutenant he served in a regiment that operated for lands of France. He walked silently to a table and spread out a huge map on it. Then he turned to Wahrenfels, took a seat across from him, and offered him a cigarette.

"We have to talk" he said. He was a man of few words and an intelligent and abstracted expression ". It is not necessary for me to detail the preliminaries of the matter, since you yourself have just suffered its consequences. In short: the Russians have put the Leningrad-Sestrorjezc railway back into operation, which our aviation had managed to destroy almost completely, and ammunition and material trains are running on it again. The thick artillery fires again on our positions. This indicates the possibility of the enemy preparing for an offensive action, trying to free itself from the encirclement or to lighten it as much as possible.

He was silent for a few minutes, puffing on his cigarette. Lieutenant Wahrenfels listened carefully.

"As you know, from Sestrorjezc, on the banks of the Ladoga, communication is established with the rest of the country not yet subdued by our weapons. The danger that this implies for our future security is evident. If weapons and supplies begin to flow into the city, Leningrad may find itself in a position to attempt a grand-style operation which we cannot in any way allow. The whole problem lies, then, in the elimination of this railway, but in an effective and complete way, without leaving the enemy the possibility of rebuilding it until the low temperatures of winter make the undertaking impossible.

Lieutenant Wahrenfels leaned back in his chair. He was beginning to like the prospect.

"Aircraft attacks" continued the colonel "are always somewhat imprecise. This time we can't leave anything to chance. In a conference held this morning with the divisional Headquarters, we agreed that the most effective thing was to send a patrol that, saving as many obstacles as possible, reaches the railway line and places powerful explosives in various places on it, covering as much extension as possible. . It is not hidden from me that the task is tiring and risky, but your patrol can do it, Lieutenant. We believe that it is the only one with the powers to do so. The election is an honor for you.

The colonel went to the table and motioned for Lieutenant Wahrenfels to come closer. The huge map of the sector ran from the Gulf of Finland to Lake Ladoga and showed in great detail the narrow strip of land on which the city is located. He took a ruler and continued:

"Pay attention, Lieutenant. Our project is the following. If you have any questions, please clarify them. As you can see, the first line comes from Pertehof and passing over Pushkin continues to Schlüsselburg. The fourth company of the second battalion is precisely there "he indicated with the ruler a place on the plane, near Pchira. By that position you will make your exit. The return ... I leave it up to you. They will carry a submachine gun with the corresponding ammunition, "submachine guns", mango and egg hand bombs, hoe and supplies in concentrated form for four or five days. Do not recklessly expose yourself. Calculate all your strokes accurately. Act preferably at night. Hide during the day and try to rest. Don't forget alarm rockets in case you need them on your return. Prepare well all day tomorrow. At eight o'clock at night, a truck will drive them to the front line. Do not lose sight of the tremendous importance of your task and bear in mind that the entire division will follow its development with the most absolute trust placed in you.

They had both risen, Lieutenant Wahrenfels replied:

"I am grateful on behalf of myself and my group for the confidence to which you have just alluded and be assured that we will know how to make it creditors.

He squared himself stiffly, and the colonel shook his hand.

"Good luck, Lieutenant. Is everything clear?

"Perfectly, my colonel, you, have explained the problem to us in general lines. Leave our account details.

He smiled and, turning around, left the room. The same car that had brought him took him back to Novo-Litka across the rolling plain where trees raised their bare branches to the sky. But the lieutenant wasted no time contemplating the panorama. His brain had been working tirelessly from the moment the colonel had sent for him.

The mission that had just been entrusted to him was a tremendous responsibility for him. A failure meant the intensification of the Russian defenses, and the winter, already approaching, hid dark and vague threats. The operation would have to be prepared with extraordinary care, leaving nothing to chance.

In the direction of the front you could hear the thunder of artillery crushing the enemy defenses. The driver pointed to the left without slowing the car. Several squadrons of planes flew in formation. Lieutenant Wahrenfels watched with his field twins. They were "Ju 87" bombers accompanied by a strong escort of very fast and powerful "Messerchmidts 109".

"It seems they are heading towards the city" said the driver.

"Indeed. The front cheers up, huh, boy? It was about time after so many months of war of position. This bores anyone.

"You never have time to be bored, my lieutenant. Sometimes it makes me want to drop this damn car and ask to join a scouting patrol, like yours.

"Driving a car has its merit too, my friend. Especially in certain special circumstances ... And it seems to me that these are going to present themselves very soon for you.

The ruins of the town were already outlined on the road. They entered the main street, free of debris, but still hard at work, clearing ruins and clearing the ground. The car stopped at what had been the patrol's quarters. All kinds of supplies were piled up in front of the door.

"Well, boy" said the lieutenant to the driver, we have arrived. Goodbye ... and if possible in Leningrad.

The driver saluted. His car made a sharp curve and drove away again in the direction of where it had come from.

The grenadiers had conditioned what was left of the premises in the best possible way. Sacks were hung in front of the windows and the walls had been propped up. The "feldwebel" came to give the news, to his lieutenant.

"Everyone ready for an operation. I will review first thing in the morning. They will spend the day preparing. The armament has to be greased, ammunition prepared and the bomb fuses checked. Take care of all this and put Corporal Schäfer in order to take care of the supply. Concentrated rations for five days. Let no one forget his "iron ranch". We will leave for positions at eight. No distractions or distractions.

The feldwebel saluted. It was serious this time. Judging from the boss's attitude, it was a major task. He had the men trained, and communicated the order received.

"I already wanted to leave this damn town" Bert commented cheerfully.

"This is our thing! "Alf added." Nothing to catch Russians like rabbits, but to assault with energy, courage and determination. This time they will find out who Alf Voss is! Ra, ta, ta, ta! He did, brandishing an imaginary 'submachine gun'.

"The festival is going to start" he said. Rudi ". And we will be in charge of preparing the fireworks with which it begins. This time we are going to have fun, I assure you.

And he tightened his belt, feeling the pistol that hung from it.

CHAPTER XII

At the first dawn of the morning, the group formed in the street. The feldwebel Engerling, with his brown face, Corporal Schäfer, silent and calm, the two servants of the machine gun, Rudi, Alf and Bert and the other four grenadiers, all rigid and firm, with their polished boots, their clean helmets and the penetrating and energetic gaze fixed on his boss. Lieutenant Wahrenfels gave them a thorough review, sparing not even the buttons on the warriors, and then proceeded to explain the scope and purpose of the raid. The grenadiers listened with the utmost attention.

"We will need to be cunning as foxes. No recklessness or useless risks. Perfect coordination and a lot of discipline. Personal action will be advisable only in cases of real trouble. I trust your intelligence and your decision. The High Command and the entire Division have their eyes on us... I won't tell you more. Everyone be here at seven thirty, ready to go.

* * *

At three in the afternoon Corporal Schäfer appeared with two soldiers loaded with sacks, proceeding to distribute the cold supply. Each grenadier received a canned bread, several cans of concentrated food, butter, which they placed in a plastic box for the purpose, vitaminized candies and a bottle of "vodka" with a snap closure. The canteens were filled with strong tea. The side bag was full. If possible, other food should be procured in enemy territory. This constituted the essential reserve for the four or five days that the raid lasted.

Everyone busied themselves with the preparations and at four in the afternoon they could be considered finished. The teams were stacked in perfect order. Corporal Schäfer had just reassembled his submachine gun, which he had cleaned and reworked piece by piece, and proceeded to apply sulfur powders to the wire drive. Rudi approached him.

71

"I'm going to get to old Ivan's tavern" he said. If the feldwebel asks for me, tell him I'll be away for a few minutes.

"Look, Rudi, don't play jokes" remiss the disgruntled corporal.

"It won't take me two minutes. It's just a matter of exchanging a few words with ...

"Yes, with your blonde, I already knew. Well go. But if they ask about you, I don't know anything. I don't feel like winning a package because of such a stubborn man. Bah! Those women...! He growled dismissively.

Rudi looked left and right. Alf and Bert were watching him. They had expected the event to occur for quite some time. They waved their hand at him, signaling him to hurry up, winking at him. He could trust them. They were the best comrades in the world.

Katia was inside the dilapidated house, fixing as much as possible some damage that would make it habitable again. Old Ivan was nailing some boards. Taking advantage of a moment when he was facing away, he made a sign to the young woman, and she went out into the street.

"I have to talk to you" said the grenadier.

"Not now. Have you not seen the work that awaits us? If we waste time, we will have a terrible winter. The openings must be covered so that air does not penetrate through them.

"We have to talk" repeated Rudi, inflexible.

"Good. Whatever you want. But not for long. My father will be angry.

They walked along the road to the exit of the town. Once near the spruce grove, Rudi stopped, took her by the arms, and gazed at her for a long time in silence.

"What's wrong with you, Rudi? Are you leaving again?

Yes, Katia. But now we will stay away for a few days ... or maybe weeks. It all depends on how things are given to us.

"Oh Rudi! She exclaimed, pressing her face against his chest.

Rudi shook it tightly.

"This time I don't have them all with me. Also, I have heard that they plan to evacuate the town. So it's not easy for us to come back here for rest.

"I knew it. My father and I have decided to move to Krasnovardeisk, with relatives, in case the order becomes effective.

"Our return here is doubtful. Anyway on my return ... if nothing happens to me, I will ask permission and go to see you in Krasnovardeisk. Don't forget to give me the addresses of those relatives of yours.

Katia shuddered.

"I have a feeling. It seems to me as if this separation is final for both of us.

Rudi laughed, forcedly.

"You already know that my patrol is the lucky patrol. We always come back, Katia, and this time there is no reason to suppose otherwise. My only regret is having to spend a few days without seeing you. Upon our return we will meet in the city. We will go to eat at a restaurant and walk in the park like that day ... remember? It will still be better than here.

Katia was crying silently.

"Come on, Katia. Do not be silly. This town is already uninhabitable. You need to move to a safer place. Also, in the city you will always be more fun, don't you think?

"More fun? Without you? Oh Rudi! Don't talk nonsense "and she redoubled her sobs.

Rudi lifted her tear-wet face and kissed her long.

"I have to go, Katia. There are severe orders and I don't want to compromise my friends.

She pressed more against his body.

"No, Rudi, no! Do not go. If something happened to you, I would die. You can be sure.

"Nothing of that. In a few days we will be together again. Come on, don't cry anymore. Give me a kiss and... "auf wieder sehen."

They walked to the entrance of the town holding each other by the waist. Katia turned to the grenadier.

"'Auf wieder sehen'" he said in German. And he ran home without turning his head. Rudi remained absorbed for a few moments and then started back towards the barracks, not without taking some precautions first.

The departure time was approaching. Some soldiers belonging to other units had come to say goodbye to the grenadiers and outside the door of the accommodation reigned unusual animation.

The night was approaching. A motorcyclist liaison crossed the street on his way to the front. Shortly after, several trucks appeared at the opposite end of the town, and while the vehicles were refueling gasoline, the soldiers who were traveling in them got out to stretch their legs a bit. Rudi thought with disgust of the compliments Katia would hear during his absence. He gritted his teeth.

At seven thirty sharp Lieutenant Wahrenfels appeared. He had substituted his hat for his helmet and was wearing full field gear. Pistol at the belt, ammunition in abundance, binoculars, canteen and bag with provisions. The silver four-pointed star gleamed on his shoulder pads. The grenadiers quickly formed and a voice of the "feldwebel" stood at attention.

"All in order? Asked the lieutenant.

"Everything in order" replied the "feldwebel", briefly.

The lieutenant gave the group an overview. The truck was waiting nearby. He made a sign, and the patrol turned to him. The feldwebel, the corporal, and the nine grenadiers climbed up one after another, placing their explosive charges in a safe place. The lieutenant took a seat in the cabin next to the driver.

"Go ahead! "shout.

The vehicle started with the loud thunder of its powerful engine. Beneath the canvas cover, Rudi scanned the road. At the exit of the town, a female figure, almost hidden among the trees, remained motionless, watching the truck pass by. Rudi blew her a kiss with his hand, and she replied in the same way, muttering:

"Bye, Rudi...! See you around!"

The truck sped up. The figure grew smaller until it disappeared into the shadows. Rudi lit a cigarette, stretched out my legs, and made himself as comfortable as possible for the short journey.

CHAPTER XIII

The passage of the enemy lines was carried out in the middle of an almost absolute darkness and without difficulties. The twelve men slipped like ghostly shadows over the sandbags, one after another, without a sound, staring straight ahead. The lieutenant marched in the lead and covered the rear, the "feldwebel" with the cocked machine pistol. The others had placed their magazines in position as they left their own trenches and were carrying a hand pump with the cord free so that it could be used as quickly as possible, at any given moment.

No one was hiding that the risk of the operation was tremendous and the responsibility very great. However, they were already used to the task and acted with extraordinary composure, without losing their nerves or worrying unnecessarily.

The front-line Russian trenches were being left behind. The precautions redoubled. Some secondary trenches had to be cleared and at any moment they ran the risk of running into a patrol or suddenly hitting the command post of a company, a supply depot or a quartermaster warehouse, whose sentries were watching the night, attentive to everyone. the rumors.

Lieutenant Wahrenfels carried in the transparent wallet that hung from his waist, a very detailed map of the sector, in which the possible places where the surveillance was special had been marked with red pencil, according to data provided by the prisoners captured a few days earlier. It was necessary to take long detours and never lose the sense of direction. Every now and then, at his gesture, they all stopped, and then, taking the small luminous precision compass from his warrior's upper pocket, he proceeded to consult it carefully.

He, as well as the feldwebel and the corporal, had a square-shaped lantern hanging from their harness, with a device by means of which the color of the light was easily changed, and which under certain circumstances could render invaluable services.

They continued their march dragging you. Some rumors sounded. In the distance you could make out the dull glow of some vehicle headlights on the roads close to the front. The city of Leningrad was on his left. In front they had Kolpino, with its factories dismantled by the bombings, and further away, to the right, Tosna, an important nucleus, on the Leningrad-Novgorod highway.

Bert, Alf, and Rudi walked one behind the other, their senses keen and their finger on the trigger of their gun. Some rockets soared into the air, briefly illuminating the surroundings. The grenadiers stood motionless, waiting for the glow to fade, then continued their slow, weary march. Over the horizon, antiaircraft machine guns fired their trails of tracer bullets skyward. The artillery fired on the Russian rear, looking for the newly installed batteries, which showed no signs of life. Above the clouds you could hear the sound of aircraft flying very high.

Suddenly, the lieutenant stopped, remaining completely still, glued to the ground. The others followed suit.

"What will happen? Bert muttered.

"We'll know right now," Alf replied. When the lieutenant stops it is because he has seen something important.

A group of three Russians advanced in the darkness. His boots made a dull sound on the hard ground.

"Quiet" the lieutenant whispered.

The Russians were already very close. They were advancing along a path that ran a few meters from the place where the men of the patrol were. One of them stopped suddenly and listened. Without a doubt, he had sensed something suspicious. Rudi was a very short distance from him. To his right rose a kind of shed. He slowly rose to his feet, concealed against one of the walls. His comrades looked at him dumbfounded. What was that madman going to do? They all put their right hands on the hilt of the machete. There was no doubt that the Russian had noticed the presence of human beings by the shed. The moments were of unsustainable tension. Throwing himself on the

Russian and his two companions was equivalent to provoking a fight capable of discovering them in a few seconds if only some other soldier was in the vicinity. However, there was no choice. Suddenly and to the shock of the entire patrol, Rudi said aloud, with perfectly natural intonation:

Pojalui poidiate doid.

The Russian stopped. He breathed loudly.

"Vozmiome zontik" he replied laughing. Dobrai notchi.

And he walked away with his two companions. The lieutenant let out a deep sigh of relief, which the others followed suit. When they were far from the dangerous place, he delayed a few meters to shake hands with Rudi.

"Good job, boy" he told him briefly, returning to the head of the column.

They had reached a road in very bad condition, which was lost in the distance, swallowed by darkness. In the distance some lights shone from some barracks. The lieutenant ordered them to continue along the shore, away from the ditch for about ten meters. This road led to the main road, which headed north toward the railroad.

"We are on the right track," he said at last. If we don't stumble, we'll reach our goal tomorrow.

"We have to cross a bridge over the Neva, my lieutenant. It will be one of the most dangerous moments, because there is no doubt that the Russians will have sentinels posted at the entrance and exit of it.

"We'll see how we can solve it. It is best to always act according to the circumstances advise. Plans conceived in advance are of no use.

The patrol walked with a little more relief. The flat terrain made it easy to walk, and it was all about keeping your eyes open so as not to be surprised by an approaching vehicle or patrol on the road. The "feldwebel" turned constantly, fulfilling its mission to protect the rear.

The rumors from the front were being left behind and a great calm enveloped the atmosphere. Yet behind that apparent sense of relief lurked the ever-constant danger of being discovered by some unforeseen sentinel. Before his eyes appeared a small group of "isbas", located on both sides of the road. The lieutenant consulted his map.

"Loditzi" he murmured.

They made a detour to avoid the houses. In one of them, a group of Russians sang loudly. Several trucks were visible in front of the door. When the grenadiers were already a few meters away, one of the trucks started up. The headlights came on suddenly and a shaft of yellowish light flashed past the lieutenant, who had just enough time to duck before being discovered. A voice harshly rebuked the reckless driver, who hastened to turn off the headlights and replace them with security ones, which only illuminated the ground a few meters away from the engine.

"That individual's foolishness has nearly cost us dear," Lieutenant Wahrenfels muttered.

"But it gave me an idea" added Rudi, coming closer. Why don't we take one of those trucks out of them and that way we can carry on a little more rested?

The lieutenant thought deeply for a moment.

"Magnificent! "He finally exclaimed." But before you go to inspect what happens in the house.

One of the grenadiers approached cautiously. In five minutes he was back.

"Most of them are drunk and several are sleeping on the floor," he said.

The group approached the vehicles, and while two grenadiers pointed their "submachine guns" at the door, the others got into one of them. Bert took the wheel.

"Ready? "Those posted in front of the house came up last.

The truck started with a jerk. Inside the "isba" the uproar continued.

"Better catch up with the truck in front. Wherever they pass, we will pass "said the lieutenant.

Bert stepped on the gas. Before long, a red light appeared in front of him.

"Stay close to him," Wahrenfels stated. And the vehicle followed in the footsteps of its predecessor, whose driver still did not seem free from the vapors of the alcohol ingested shortly before.

CHAPTER XIV

"It is very little until dawn" said the lieutenant. If we got to the bridge early enough, we might get the truck across it better than on foot.

"Those there" answered Bert, pointing with his chin forward "are convinced that we are his companions who have decided at the last minute to leave the" isba "and continue the march.

"Let's trust our lucky stars" said the lieutenant.

The mighty Neva, a river that runs through the city of Leningrad from part to part, flowing into the Gulf of Finland, was no longer very far. Crossing it was the first stage of the operation. On the other side it would be easier to operate, because there are fewer military precautions due to the considerable distance from the front line.

The march continued for an hour. The coolness of the mighty stream of water was noticeable in the air.

"The bridge! Bert suddenly exclaimed, pointing to a confused shadow rising in front of them.

The patrol chief raised the rear curtain and warned the boys:

"Everyone calm and silent, as if you were sleeping. Rudi, go into the booth.

The vehicle slowed for a moment and Rudi took a seat at the right side of the window. They remained glued to the front truck. At the entrance of the bridge a voice exclaimed:

"Stoi !.

The first vehicle slowed and its driver stuck his head out the window.

"We are returning from transporting ammunition to the front" he told the sentry. Some trucks have stayed overnight in Loditzi.

Rudi, who had taken off his helmet, lowered the window glass and added:

"Go! Hurry up, we can't wait to get home!

"Good. Go ahead "said the Russian.

And the two trucks passed him, slowly. Rudi still had a second to say to the sentry as he raised the glass again:

"Dobroi notchi, tovarich.

The lieutenant smiled, muttering:

"The thing is going. Now comes a very flat and depopulated region. We will continue in the vehicle until the day approaches, and then we will leave it somewhere that does not arouse suspicion.

"What a pity! "Rudi exclaimed. Dawn was near. As they reached a bend in the road, they saw a village.

"If the one in front continues, we will stay at the exit. In this way they will think that we have stopped to rest a little.

They did so, leaving the vehicle separated between two houses. They got out with the greatest stealth and were lost in the still very dense shadows of the night.

The railroad was close now. As soon as the morning light made it impossible to walk in the open, they sought a refuge in which to take a well-deserved rest. Nearby they saw some abandoned hovels, in front of which were great piles of blackened straw. They went to them and hid themselves in the best possible way between the straw and the squalid walls. The lieutenant called his "feldwebel."

"Distribute the guards, and let everyone sleep.

They grouped together occupying the smallest possible space and the first supplier stood as a sentry, observing the surroundings with caution. They would be relieved every hour. The others tried to settle into the straw. They dug up their provisions and ate a bite. Then each one lay down in the most comfortable position.

At noon a loud noise woke them up. The lieutenant stood slightly alarmed. Everyone was staring at the road. About three miles away a caravan of trucks had just come to a halt and its occupants were rapidly scattering across the field. A squad of "Messerchmidts" attacked the trucks with their machine guns.

"Nobody move from your place! "Ordered the lieutenant, amid the din produced by the clatter of the machines and the hum of the engines.

The planes made several passes, swift as lightning, spewing fire and shooting down everything in their path. The occupants of the trucks fled in terror. Some of them took refuge in holes located a short distance from the place occupied by the grenadiers. They gazed enthusiastically at the work of their own, but without losing sight of the Russians, at whom they pointed their weapons.

"As long as they don't think of machine-gunning the houses, believing that there are troops in them," said Bert.

"We'd do a good deal," Alf declared, staring into the air.

The planes finally moved away, losing themselves on the horizon.

"Those clumsy ones almost killed us," said the corporal, observing the trails produced by the bullets a very short distance from his shelter.

The Russian trucks started up again. Two of them were left on the road and a good number of wounded were collected and transported to one of the vehicles.

"It seems that they have had aim" commented the lieutenant.

"Everything that you want. But can you imagine the result of a good charge of dynamite placed in the very middle of the formation? Asked Rudi, unwilling to admit the effectiveness of that procedure.

From that moment on, no one slept anymore. It was eaten briefly and Lieutenant Wahrenfels proceeded to give some instructions, as the placement of the first charge would take place that night.

They left at dusk. The railroad was barely two kilometers away. They came crawling across the rough terrain. The slope rose dark and threatening. The trains ran widely spaced. The corporal mounted his submachine gun, and the two servants took up positions on either side, boxes ready. Two grenadiers advanced with explosive charges fitted with delayed fuzes. Its operation had been calculated for two hours later, allowing time for the others to be placed. All three would explode at approximately the same time, destroying several kilometers of track, so completely that their repair would be almost impossible in the short space of time that remained for the onset of winter.

The charges were perfectly hidden with stones and earth. The patrol followed the track, walking on both sides, alert and keen-eyed. The second load was placed. The road curved in that place. They were about to place the third when the lieutenant stopped his boys. An iron bridge was visible in the distance. The lieutenant stared at him with sparkling eyes.

"Tall! "Ordered." We will reserve the third and fourth charges for something better. Do you see the bridge? If we sink it, the possibilities of circulation in this way will be completely eliminated in several months.

But you must hurry, my lieutenant. The other two loads are already working "indicated the" feldwebel-bel "". We can't waste a second, and there are most likely sentries at the entrance and exit.

"And what are we here for? Rudi said, pointing to himself and his two companions.

"Go ahead, guys," the lieutenant commanded.

Rudi, Alf, and Bert slithered like reptiles, wielding their machetes. The first sentry was perfectly distinguishable, wrapped in his cloak. The three grenadiers went down the slope until they almost touched the water's edge. The steel mass towered above their heads in its convoluted frame. They climbed alongside the metal beams. The sound of the water eliminated his footsteps. The first sentinel fell with an accurate machete blow. The second had a moment of alarm, but before he could cry out a hand grabbed his throat and Bert brought him down with his hoe. They returned to inform the rest of the patrol that the road was clear.

Four grenadiers proceeded to place the charges on the weak points of the bridge, while the others stood guard. The task took longer than expected because of how difficult it was to carry out, due to the prevailing darkness. The lieutenant consulted his watch. It was just a short time before the first and second charges exploded. And before that happened, she needed to have the others in place and gotten far enough away to be safe. The boys worked feverishly, securing the sticks of dynamite with wire. Suddenly the feldwebel stiffened, listened intently, and crouching down, put one ear to the rail.

"A train is coming! "He announced, unable to contain a slight nervousness.

"You have to hurry! Ordered the lieutenant.

CHAPTER XV

At last the grenadiers returned one after another. The charges were set, almost to zero. The time of the explosion was approaching.

"To the race! "Ordered the head of the patrol.

They ran down the slope, missing over the rocks and sinking their boots into the mud, which splashed around them, splashing their faces.

The train was approaching. They ran for more than a kilometer. At last, at a signal from the lieutenant, they fell gasping to the ground. They took cover behind an eminence of the ground and waited with nerves on the verge of exploding. There were a few minutes before the charges exploded. The convoy consisted of a good number of wagons.

"What if they had ammunition, my lieutenant? "Asked Rudi." What fireworks!

"In this case, our task would be complete. But will we be so lucky?

"In a very short time we will know," said the 'feldwebel'. If only the charges didn't fail!

The silence was complete. The locomotive had already passed the site of the first mine and was very close to the second. He also passed over it. He was going to enter the bridge. The black smoke from its chimney stood out against the darkness of the sky. Suddenly a horrible detonation shook the atmosphere. A dazzling flare lit up everything. Chunks of rail and huge boulders were scattered through the air in a cloud of very black smoke, and as they began to slam to the ground, the second mine exploded, catching the last of the wagons squarely. At the same moment, the locomotive reared as if lifted by a gigantic hand, turned on itself and collapsed on its side amid an indescribable roar, while the bridge sank, its supports broken by dynamite, between a mass of twisted girders and cement, between overpowering creaks. One of the front carriages flew with a dull crash, contributing to the total destruction. The work could be considered perfect. The lieutenant and his boys watched the spectacle with clenched fists and blazing eyes.

Great flames rose from the scene of the accident. The cars burned with a pungent smell.

"Let's not waste time" said the head of the patrol. You have to get out of here as soon as possible. Do you want us to be surprised by contemplating our own feat?

The group mobilized. You had to move away in forced marches to avoid being caught by the Russians. Some searchlights had begun to come on and there was the distant roar of vehicles.

"For now they think it was aviation," said Bert. But it won't take long for them to discover the truth. When it does, we'd better be well away from here.

They ran across the country without stopping for a moment, possessed by the desire to put as much ground space as possible between them and catastrophe.

Suddenly, Lieutenant Wahrenfels, who was in the lead, stopped making frantic gestures. Everyone slowed down. In front of them, quite far away, patrols were approaching at a brisk pace. The grenadiers were grouped in a small hollow, while the Russians passed on both sides uttering denunciations. When they reached the road, they ducked into the ditch. Two trucks and some ambulances were coming.

"In a few minutes the news will have spread throughout this sector," said the lieutenant. Escape will be difficult, boys. It will be necessary to gather courage and cold blood. Let us follow the road, always keeping our distance from it.

"The worst thing will be to cross the river" said Rudi. As we do not swim ...!

"We should have a good bath," Alf added, "after what we've sweated running.

To the right, Russian 15.5 batteries had started firing. The flashes followed one another rhythmically and the whistle of the projectiles was perceived on their journey towards the German trenches.

"Why don't we fly them too, my lieutenant? Asked Rudi.

"Stop joking around and don't lose sight of the ground you are on! The one admonished him.

They advanced at a rapid pace. The lieutenant got his bearings. The river was not far. There was a certain coolness in the air.

"Don't even think about crossing the bridge," said the head of the patrol. They will have redoubled their vigilance.

"How much fun we had on the way out! Alf exclaimed.

"How grateful my feet would be to find a good truck! A grenadier murmured.

"We will rest on the other side.

The slope was beginning. In a little while they perceived the shine of the water. The bulk of the bridge rose a short distance away. A group of soldiers guarded the entrance. The possibility of eliminating them by means of a good burst of the submachine gun and passing over everything was discussed, but the lieutenant was of the opinion of continuing to maintain prudence. The best thing was to explore the shores. Perhaps there was a way to cross the river without the Russians noticing. In this case, they would keep an active watch, believing them on the other side and their withdrawal would be easier.

They hid among the herbs. The "feldwebel" dispatched three grenadiers to survey the surroundings. The boys walked away in silence. Shortly after they were back at full throttle.

"There is a boat a very short distance from here," they reported.

"Can we all fit? Asked the lieutenant.

"I doubt it. And even more carrying the weapons and the two boxes of ammunition "was the response of the grenadier.

"In this case we will go through two stages.

The lieutenant, the corporal, and five soldiers climbed into the weak boat, which rocked dangerously and nearly capsized. Alf, Bert, Rudi, two more grenadiers and the "feldwebel" waited their turn on the shore. The minutes passed slowly, as the boat sped away, propelled by the oars. It took him more than half an hour to get back. The six grenadiers climbed with great caution to the light boat, overloaded. They had barely started rowing when shouts sounded from the shore.

"You have to hurry! "Said Rudi." It seems to me that we have been discovered.

The oars plunged into the water hurriedly and the boat moved faster.

"We'd better go with the flow a bit to throw them off their feet," advised Alf.

The boat advanced on a steep diagonal. Flares flashed on the shore and bullets began to whistle.

"If we manage to stay in the same direction, we would be already liquidated" said a grenadier, observing the small jets that raised the projectiles.

They rowed with renewed vigor. The shore was already close. They docked downstream from where the first half of the patrol did. The lieutenant was frankly concerned. Finally, one of the boys announced:

"Here they come!

The two groups met.

"Things are getting ugly, my lieutenant" said Rudi, wiping his forehead with his handkerchief. Those bullets do not bode well.

"The outlook has worsened, indeed" agreed the lieutenant, "but it is not hopeless. The worst thing is that the day is approaching. We will have to advance across the country without worrying about clarity. Just in case we will take off our helmet and wear it hanging from our belt.

They continued walking, in a tight group. The clarity grew greater every moment. The lieutenant did not want to stop to rest until the distance between them and the river increased as much as possible. Finally, at noon he gave the stop sign. A short distance away, some "isbas" were observed. The lieutenant observed them with his field cufflinks:

"They are occupied by soldiers" he said. We will have to make a detour.

"More detours? Rudi complained.

"Watch out! Body to ground! "Ordered the" feldwebel. "

A squad of horsemen galloped across the plain. You could see their leather caps and the rifles they carried on their shoulders.

"If they have launched patrols all over the county, I see something difficult to get out of this trap" said Bert.

"There is nothing difficult for the Wahrenfels patrol," said Rudi. Engrave this in your memory: We have to go back, do you hear ...? And we will return.

CHAPTER XVI

They made a long detour to avoid the "isbas" and they were left behind after a long walk. They were heading into swampy terrain. Tall grasses grew everywhere and the air was foul and foul.

"Good place for an ambush" said a grenadier.

"From them to us... or the other way around? Asked Rudi.

"I don't think we have time to prepare it" intervened the lieutenant. Open your eyes wide and no distractions. I don't like this terrain at all.

They were following a barely perceptible path. To the right and left, the soft earth sank under his feet. Suddenly, the lieutenant, who was marching in the lead, stopped, waving his hand. The feldwebel approached. In front of them, a patrol was camped, resting. There would be about twenty men, fierce-looking and fierce, their heads covered with a tall fur cap.

"Cossacks" said the "feldwebel" in a low voice.

"We cannot change our path or make a detour" declared the lieutenant, after a few moments of reflection. On the other hand, going back is impossible. Are you determined?

The grenadiers nodded. Rudi stroked his machete. Alf and Bert wielded two hand pumps. The others, lined up the group with their "submachine guns."

"Noise or no noise? Asked Rudi.

The "feldwebel" now pointed forward. On the nearby road a stationary truck could be seen.

"Go for them and for the truck! "It was the concise order of Lieutenant Wahrenfels." It all depends on falling on the group by surprise.

At a signal from their commander, the grenadiers attacked as one man, firing their 'submachine guns'. Two Russians fell. The others managed to rally and, forming a tight nucleus, went on to a desperate defense. The grenadiers took up their machetes. There was no choice but to win or die. The fight began fiercely by both sides, between denunciations and exclamations of fury. Rudi roared, squeezing his opponent's neck until his knuckles ached. The Russian tried to trip him, but he nimbly avoided it and, tensing the powerful muscles of his arms, knocked him to the ground. His machete rose into the air twice, stained with blood. The other grenadiers fought like lions.

"Don't let any of them get away! The lieutenant yelled, amid the reigning chaos. Blows and machetes echoed with tragic murmur. One of the Russians had taken his rifle. Bert rushed at him and, snatching him away, delivered a tremendous blow to the head. The Cossack gave a low groan as he collapsed. He clicked a short burst. Alf had just eliminated three opponents who had come within range. The feldwebel was methodically firing his pistol, without missing a single projectile, as if he were in a contest.

Only four Russians put up resistance, but it was short-lived. Twenty corpses littered the ground. Some of the grenadiers were wounded, although fortunately only slightly. There wasn't a minute to waste.

"To the truck! Ordered the lieutenant.

Bert threw himself behind the wheel, Rudi jumped in beside him, pointing his "submachine gun" out the window. The lieutenant did the same, with his pistol cocked. The grenadiers had rushed to the rear. Corporal Schäfer placed his submachine gun on the cockpit and attached a tape.

The truck started up and within seconds it was at breakneck speed. They passed a group of houses. Glancing back, Alf could see some people coming out of the gates, gazing at the rampant vehicle in amazement. The patrol's salvation depended on the engine not failing or running out of fuel.

After a scramble in the road, which Bert recklessly took, kicking up a cloud of dust and making the wheels squeak, a large group of soldiers suddenly appeared, perhaps a company, blocking it completely,

Bert stepped on the accelerator. An officer gave a few hasty orders. The corporal pulled the trigger. The machine rattled from its precarious location and a spray of bullets sowed death and panic in the ranks of the Russians, opening a gap through which the vehicle shot through. Two machine guns answered, but the bullets did not cause any damage.

"This is working first! Rudi yelled excitedly.

The lieutenant was looking straight ahead, scowling. It was not hidden from him that the dangers were becoming almost insurmountable. The news that a German exploration patrol had just blown up the bridge and the railroad would have already circulated like wildfire. All the posts would be warned and the crossing of the Russian lines would end up becoming a company of titans.

The first houses of a town suddenly appeared. The lieutenant studied the map.

"Loditzi" he said. Don't you remember?

"I think so! "Exclaimed Bert." Do we stop for a drink?

"It will be necessary to abandon this truck as soon as we are five or six kilometers from the town," announced the lieutenant.

"A shame! "Rudi lamented." With what I liked this race!

After the last few houses, Bert slowly slowed down. The gas tank was almost empty now. A cloud of smoke billowed from the radiator. He pushed the truck into some bushes and the grenadiers jumped to the ground.

"Phew! "Alf gasped." I'd rather deal with the Russians than with this devilish Bert.

Everyone took advantage of the brief respite to take a drink from their canteen. Thirst burned their throats from the dust swallowed during the frenzy of flight.

"From now on we will continue with the utmost precautions" said the lieutenant. The lines are close, and in them the enemy will have established the maximum vigilance. We will hide until nightfall, and we will undertake the last stage of our mission.

They were hiding between some cracks in the ground and while two grenadiers watched, the others tried to head off a brief sleep. In the late afternoon, the lieutenant proceeded to an inspection of the weapons and supplies. They still had enough ammunition left, the rockets were intact, and they still carried their bomb supply. The wounded grenadiers had been bandaged with their field dressings and could hold out to the end. The lieutenant recommended gathering strength for the decisive effort, not getting carried away by nerves and maintaining maximum serenity and caution at all times.

They ate the remains of their provisions and poured the leftover "vodka" into their canteens in order to dispose of the bottles.

At eight o'clock Lieutenant Wahrenfels gave the order to march. The weary grenadiers tried not to let down their forces. The ultimate success of his mission depended on it. It was necessary to maintain the energies until the moment when they crossed their own lines again. The advance began without precipitation. In the distance, the glow of rockets could be perceived and the muffled sound of the shooting reached his ears. The lieutenant marched ahead with his compass in hand, serene and impassive.

They were in the very dangerous rearguard sector, close to the front lines, where services are established and where at every moment you can run into sentries or patrols.

The lieutenant stopped. The others joined him. He waved his hand forward. "That's the address," he murmured. The view to the front ... and whatever it takes, you have to go through.

CHAPTER XVII

Rudi approached the lieutenant with a bundle in his hand. It was a Russian cloak that he had found abandoned next to a barrack.

"Maybe it can help us" he whispered.

The sentries were more and more numerous. Their silhouettes were perceived in some places and voices were everywhere asking for the password.

The patrol stopped in the shelter of some houses, and Rudi pricked up his ears, trying to distinguish the precious word that at a given moment could mean the door of their desired freedom opening before them. Two soldiers passed a very short distance. One of them was speaking. Rudi paid attention.

"How is it "...? Oh yeah! Bostok Zapade. I had forgotten.

"Good. I already caught it "muttered Rudi, once they had passed.

The trenches were already close. The shooting sounded close and the rockets were perceived rising from the other side.

They followed an evacuation ditch, with the "submachine guns" ready. They went in single file, somewhat spaced apart. The ditch was very shallow and at one point they could jump out to safety. Two sentries outlined his silhouette at close range. Just beyond was the main trench and behind it, no-man's-land.

"If we finish with those we can consider the game won" murmured the lieutenant.

Rudi put on his cape. He strode forward in the direction of one of them.

"Tall! Who goes The password!

"Bostok Zapade" Rudi replied, approaching. Once before the sentry, he pointed his gun at his belly while adding ". Tell the other one to come closer.

The terrified Russian obeyed. His companion advanced towards them. Rudi jumped back and covering the two of them with his "submachine gun" he waved to his companions. Bert and Alf came quickly. There were two thudding thumps. The other grenadiers had begun work on the fence, clearing a path. Once practicable, the entire group slipped to the other side. The lieutenant took a deep breath. However, it was not wise to be overconfident. You could even run into an enemy scouting patrol or expose yourself to bullets from your own machine guns. They crouched forward. The lieutenant got his bearings again. The position from which they had started was somewhat to the right. It was better not to stay any longer in this dangerous terrain.

"Let one go ahead" he indicated to the "feldwebel." He called the nearest grenadier, who advanced with great caution. A somewhat distant voice was heard shouting:

"Tall! The password!

The grenadier returned. The patrol got into motion. There was no step on the fence and they had to slide to the nearest one. At the moment of jumping into the trench Rudi exclaimed:

"This time I really thought we weren't counting it!

"What a pessimist! "Replied Bert." Well, I was sure to return. Have we ever failed?

"Silence! "Ordered the lieutenant." That we are not home yet.

He contemplated his group with pride, one more mission was accomplished. And this time, the task had been worthy of them. His colleagues from all over the sector and the High Command could calmly await the momentous moment when the offensive began that would destroy the last defenses of the besieged city. The railroad that supplied ammunition and supplies to that one would not return to circulate. The only branch that linked the populous city to the outside world had ceased to exist.

"Get going, guys. And this time we do deserve a good rest.

"If they let us enjoy it..." Rudi commented sarcastically.

Lieutenant Wahrenfels briefly interviewed the captain of the company that covered that sector from the front, giving him the news of his return. Shortly after, and in a truck that was unloading supplies, they left for the Battalion command post. Major Braun received them with the utmost cordiality. Once the lieutenant had informed him of the results, he got up, shaking his hand warmly.

"I hope" he said that the divisional High Command recognizes the merit of its task. As for me, I congratulate you with all my heart.

He had the grenadiers served coffee and put at their disposal a vehicle in which they would travel to the Battalion command post, where the lieutenant had to inform his colonel of the satisfactory results achieved in the company.

They left immediately. The little village soon appeared and while the grenadiers were staying in a nearby house, the lieutenant went towards the "isba" in which Colonel Weiss lived. When he found himself in front of his superior, he stiffened, announcing in a calm voice:

"The objective has been reached. The train track has been completely destroyed.

Colonel Weiss made him sit down, ordered his assistant to bring coffee, and begged the lieutenant:

"Tell me about the operation in all kinds of details. Truth be told, I wasn't expecting you so soon. I must not hide from you now that we have feared for your safety.

Lieutenant Wahrenfels took some time to finish his tale. No details were left. The colonel nodded his head.

"My warmest congratulations" he said at the end ", which I extend to the boys who make up his group. This time I hope that your merits will be rewarded in a way worthy of you: You will set out for Krasnovardeisk at once. The town of Novo-Litka has been evacuated. They will rest in the city for as long as the command deems appropriate and that this time may be long. It is not easy for the enemy to pester us again. Our aviation and our artillery will give a good account of these heavy-caliber pieces. On the other hand, lacking ammunition, their existence will be precarious. Now, take a short rest until daylight.

Lieutenant Wahrenfels joined his grenadiers. The most frank joy reigned in the house, which was increased even more when it was learned that they were going to the city. Few of them slept during the few hours until dawn, Rudi was thinking of Katia. Would he find her safe and sound? Had he left the city? He was willing to look for her everywhere. His love for the young woman had grown during that brief, yet extremely dangerous, separation.

They left town after having breakfast. The fields slid by on either side of the vehicle, golden in the morning sun. The grenadiers sang with joy. They passed several towns and villages, the inhabitants of which went about their usual tasks. One of the villages showed the traces of a recent attack by Russian aviation. Several "isbas" were burning.

"Apparently, they cheer up," someone said.

"It won't be for long," Alf replied. The coup has ended his last chances of resistance. I bet what you will that before winter Leningrad has been taken.

"And what front will they take us to next? Asked Bert.

"Anyone knows! "Exclaimed the corporal." Maybe we go back to the South.

"For my part, I'd rather stay here" muttered Rudi.

"Of course! Next to your blonde, right? Asked Bert dismissively.

"It's just that I'm getting fond of all this" explained Rudi, smiling.

"Brave fool! Alf exclaimed. Take a liking to this! Have you ever heard such nonsense?

They entered the outskirts of Krasnovardeisk. A sentry stopped the truck.

"It is the Wahrenfels patrol that is returning from an operation," the "feldwebel" told him.

The sentry called for another soldier.

"I have an order to take you to your accommodation," said the latter, and getting into the truck was indicating to the driver the direction to take. At last they stopped in front of a good-looking house.

"Good! "Exclaimed the lieutenant." We have finally arrived. Down with everyone ...! And try to get some rest before starting your forays around the city.

CHAPTER XVIII

That same afternoon, Rudi, set out in search of Katia. The signs that the young woman had written on a piece of paper, shortly before parting ways in Novo-Litka, indicated a street located towards one of the extreme neighborhoods. Despite his fatigue, Rudi set off.

He crossed streets and streets, through which a poorly dressed crowd roamed, and mixed with soldiers of all weapons. The restaurants and taverns were full. The animation was constant. He asked passersby for directions several times. He passed huge buildings and crossed a tree-covered ravine, which once must have been a park.

He was in the neighborhood opposite the one from which he had come. He saw a huge warehouse of war material. Tanks and cannons were wrapped in canvas covers, hardened by the cold of the night. He stopped at a corner. Katia street was very close. Kept walking. In a few minutes he was at a lively intersection. Two cafes occupied the corners. Rudi thought it might be better to have a drink and then wait in front of the house. If Katia did not come out, she would proceed to ask about her directly.

He took a seat at one of the tables on the sidewalk. He looked inside. The patrons, mostly soldiers, filled the premises. Several waitresses came and went constantly. Suddenly her heart skipped a beat.

"Katia! "shout.

The young woman was about to drop the tray she was carrying. She came running up to him. Rudi took her by the arms. Some soldiers began to murmur and smile.

"What are you doing here?

"I had to accept this job. Life in the city is very difficult ", she replied breathlessly, looking into his eyes.

"Let's go right away! We have to talk about many things!

"I will try to get permission from the owner to leave. Wait for me a bit.

It took a long time to come out. Impatience consumed Rudi, who several times was on the point of entering and rushing against the imbecile who was thus holding the girl. Finally, Katia appeared, stripped of her apron. She was wearing a simple but tasteful dress that enhanced her charms. There were traces of fatigue on his face.

"I had to get to work" he explained as soon as they had moved away a bit. My relatives are poor and they cannot support my father and me. If you only knew how I have remembered you these days! You're not leaving again, are you, Rudi?

"I hope this time they let us rest for a good season. Although we also thought so last time … and you see the things that have happened.

They went to the park, through which they had walked that day, already so far away. Katia was squeezing his arm tightly. People looked at them, curious. The tall grenadier, in his battered uniform and the beautiful young Russian woman, made an extremely attractive couple.

They took a seat in a cafe near the pond. She took him by the hand, staring at him.

"If you go away again" he said, "I think I will die.

Rudi was thoughtful.

"I will do my best to stay by your side, Katia. I understand that a transformation is taking place in me. I am not the same as before. During the combat I have your image present in my brain and I ardently wish to return safe and sound.

They got up and continued walking slowly. As they reached the water's edge, she leaned down to look at herself.

"You remember?

Rudi nodded. They kissed passionately, pressing against each other.

"Don't go," Katia repeated, sobbing. Couldn't you find some destination that would force you to stay here? Always from one place to another, exposed to all kinds of dangers! It is time for you to rest a bit ... Don't go out again, I beg you.

The sobs shook her body. Rudi drew her against him, and they both remained in that attitude for a long time, indifferent to the passage of time.

"It's time to go back", said Katia, after a while ". I had forgotten that I have a job. And that at night, it gets worse. The owner of the cafe has let me leave on the condition that I return as soon as possible. I told him it was something of the utmost importance, and he reluctantly agreed. But I can't lose that job.

Rudi clenched his jaws. He imagined Katia working in the cafe for hours on end, listening to the soldiers' pleasantries and enduring the owner's bad temper. It was necessary to put an end to this situation.

They kissed each other long and started walking. They said goodbye in a corner near the cafe. Rudi headed towards his accommodation. Suddenly, he heard a call to him. Two grenadiers from his group were sitting at a restaurant table.

"Hey, Rudi! Yen for a drink. We invite you... And look who's in there.   __

Rudi came closer. Alf and Bert were occupying another table inside.

"What a bad face you have! "Exclaimed Bert." Has beer made you feel bad?

"Of course! "Alf added." He had not drunk it for so long that he has abused it and the poor ...

"Shut up, hell! Rudi grumbled, sitting up.

The other two grenadiers approached.

"We can be together, can't we? It's getting cold out there.

The conversation became general. One of the grenadiers began to explain his interview with a girl from the auxiliary services, who was in an office of the General Staff and whom he had known for a long time.

"She is a beautiful girl" he detailed. With wavy blonde hair and... "He made an expressive gesture with both hands." They live very well here. They enjoy many advantages and, at least, they allow themselves the luxury of being clean... Although for this it is not worth being in the war, is not it? Ours is much more fun.

"And what is that young woman doing? Bert wanted to know.

"She is in charge of the supplies to the canteens distributed throughout the city and of the direction of their personnel. By the way, he explained to me that in the General Staff they suffer from a certain lack of specialized elements. The front absorbs more people every day and the offices are lacking in some essential elements. The Russian interpreter has been transferred to another place, and the general looks for one to replace him, without being able to find him. There are many who present themselves, but none speak the language of the country with the perfection required for the position.

Rudi had pricked up his ears.

"Here we have our friend Rudi," said Bert, "who dominates it wonderfully and, instead, spends his life hitting shots on enemy ground. What contrasts life has!

"What they would give to get their hands on it! "Alf added." But what would the patrol be without his help?

Rudi was absorbed in staring at his glass.

"Hey, Rudi! You have slept? Bert said, pushing him by the arm. How is your blonde ...? Because I suppose you've already seen it.

"Very well," replied the grenadier briefly, getting up and preparing to leave. Is someone coming with me?

Alf and Bert got up.

"Come on" said the first, yawning. I have a tremendous dream. I'm going to sleep well!

The three of them walked down the street ahead, their shod boots clattering to the ground. Rudi, could barely sleep that night, a thousand different ideas were intertwined in his brain. He could clearly hear the words of the grenadier: "The Russian interpreter has been transferred to another place and the general is looking for someone to replace him

...". What would his companions think of him, if they knew that he was planning to abandon them? Would they take him for a coward ...? No. That was not possible. But the image of Katia then emerged, smiling, with her blond hair and blue eyes. "There are many who show up, but ...".

He fell asleep towards dawn. He had made his decision.

CHAPTER XIX

The next morning Rudi left without telling anyone. A whirlwind of intertwined ideas troubled his brain. He directed his steps towards the offices of the General Staff. There was an incessant bustle in them. He entered the hall. On a bulletin board, he was able to read a copy of a sheet distributed to the battalion commanders ordering that investigations be carried out among the companies to find out the presence of soldiers who spoke Russian perfectly. Said soldiers should report to that Headquarters for examination. Rudi had enough of that. He returned to the barracks. The boys had spread out into the city, and only the one in charge of the watch remained.

"Have you seen the lieutenant? He asked.

"He was still here a few moments ago, but he just left.

Rudi wandered the busy streets, mired in a thousand worries. In his heart, doing this with his comrades in arms seemed like a scoundrel to him. How was the patrol going to manage without his help from then on? What would the lieutenant say when he communicated his wish to take the exam to stay in Krasnovardeisk as a common clerk? He, who had always despised that fauna so much! He was in the park and passed very close to Katia's restaurant, although without going to visit her. Why, if they couldn't go out for a walk together either? There was no choice but to wait for the night.

At noon he returned to the accommodation. The grenadiers did not come to eat. They had stayed in restaurants willing to savor delicacies they had been deprived of for a long time. The lieutenant wasn't there either, Rudi inwardly cursed his bad luck. Her nerves were on the verge of exploding. Kept around. Around five in the afternoon, he suddenly saw Lieutenant Wahrenfels crossing a street. He started after him, until he caught up with him.

"My lieutenant! "I call.

The officer stopped. Rudi walked up to him and saluted respectfully.

"What, there, boy? Wahrenfels asked, patting him on the arm. How are you lonely? And your two friends? Are you no longer the "inseparable three"?

"My lieutenant" began Rudi "would like to speak with you.

"Wow, man! What is that serious face coming to? Is something serious wrong with you? Let's go sit in that cafe.

They took a seat at a table, and the lieutenant ordered two beers.

"Good. Explain to me. You seem somewhat concerned.

"I am... The truth is that I don't know how to start... For a while now, I feel something different. Maybe it's tiredness. Good. In summary: I have seen an advertisement in the General Staff offices asking for Russian interpreters and I thought that maybe I ...

The lieutenant stared at him in puzzlement. I would never have expected such an exit.

"Well, Rudi" he replied slowly sipping his beer. You are lucky enough to have a perfect command of the language of the country, and you are perfectly entitled to try to offer your services to a higher body where they may be of more use than in our modest patrol. For my part I do not think to put any inconvenience. It is a very personal thing. However, you can be sure that we will miss you very much.

The officer got up. I was sincerely shocked.

"My lieutenant. I don't want you to think ...

"Nothing, Rudi. I wish you luck. You will inform me of how the exam went, and in case your decision is irrevocable, I will have to find you a substitute ... Well, bye.

Rudi saluted. A strong feeling of shame washed over him. He began to walk, and his steps unconsciously took him towards Katia's cafe. It was already quite late and the young woman would be about to leave. Inside the premises, the soldiers were rampaging and laughing. Rudi waited in the corner. The young woman made a sign to him through the windows. Ten minutes later she was out on the street. They held arms. Rudi was silent.

"What's the matter, Rudi? Are things not going well?

"Katia" he replied. You and I cannot live apart. If I were to leave again, I am sure I would fail in my task. Yesterday, a grenadier in my group casually explained to me that they need a good interpreter in the General Staff offices. I am "he smiled forcibly." I am going to introduce myself. Can you imagine if they admit me? I would stay in the city, maybe until the end of the war. We would not part anymore. How about? Are you not happy?

Katia was looking at him very seriously. They walked in silence for a long time.

"No, Rudi" she finally said. It would be wonderful, but you can't do it. What will your classmates say?

"What do I care...?

"No" repeated Katia. In the long run you would be ashamed to have abandoned them. You would regret your decision and your anger would turn against me. You were born to fight and you will fight to the end. I'll wait for you, do you hear me? I will wait for you because I am sure that you will have to return. Do not do that.

"I can't live without you, Katia", he replied. I am sure that in the long run it would falter, and that is even worse. Tomorrow I will take that exam. If I am lucky and they pass, I will stay in the city, I will always be able to dress clean and I will stop hearing the hiss of bullets and the roar of explosions. I look forward to a little rest. Don't you think I deserve it?

"Yes, you deserve it but not like this.

"I have thought about it very well. You know I'm a bit stubborn. My decision is irrevocable. Now ... if you don't love me ...

"Oh Rudi! "She exclaimed, pressing herself against his arm." Don't even say that ...

Their walk went on until very late. When they returned, the two walked slowly in ecstasy. Katia had allowed herself to be convinced, but deep down she anticipated a future full of threats. However, everything was overshadowed by the prospect of being able to see Rudi every day. His image forged beautiful images for the days to come when both could walk without the constant risk of a separation.

Returning to his barracks, Rudi paused at the door, hardly daring to enter. How would you communicate the news to your two comrades? Would they take her sarcasm or would they take charge of her situation?

Alf and Bert were getting ready to go to bed. Rudi hesitated for a long time. At last he said:

"I have to talk to you guys.

"Is it something serious? Asked Bert. Your face does not bode well.

"Yes. This is something serious. I have decided to stay here.

They both looked at him puzzled.

"It seemed to me" Alf commented "that the matter of the blonde could not end well.

"Call me an idiot, call me a coward or whatever you want, but I can't live without that woman.

"And where do you stay ...? But I'm already falling! "Exclaimed Bert." In the Headquarters they need a magnificent interpreter ... and you have thought that your services are essential in that place. Sure! Who knows Russian like Rudi?

"I understand that you are making fun of me. But ... that happens to you park you have never been in love.

"Well, be very happy with your Katia" said Bert "and have a lot of fun in the city ... We are leaving tomorrow afternoon.

"What, are you leaving tomorrow?

"A while ago the lieutenant told us. It seems that the front is mobilizing and that all available forces will be necessary. We do not know if it is the final assault on the city, but as you can see, our famous break could not be achieved this time either. I mean ... for you, yes.

Rudi was thoughtful. He stretched out on his mat and tried to sleep, but without succeeding until a late hour. Bert and Alf were snoring quietly into a deep sleep.

CHAPTER XX

Rudi's test was a complete success. A specialist colonel from the Information Section made him sit down at a table covered in papers. Rudi read some texts, which he then proceeded to translate. Then the other way around. At last the colonel got up and said with a satisfied air:

"To date, you are the first to show up here with an exact knowledge of the language. The only thing left to do is take the pronunciation test. If this is perfect, the square is for you.

He sent for a Russian employee at the offices.

"Can you chat for a while" he told them.

The Russian and Rudi engaged in a short, quick conversation. The Russian was nodding in surprise.

"Monoga jarosi. Monoga jarosi "he finally said addressing the lieutenant. And he added in broken German ". He speaks perfect Russian.

"What unit does it belong to?

"The Wahrenfels scouting patrol is affected by the second battalion of the third regiment," Rudi replied.

"The patrol is now on rest, right?

"Yes, my colonel. Although it seems that they will leave today for another place closer to the front.

"Indeed. Units are mobilized for a major operation ... Good. In the early afternoon the transfer order will be issued. However, if you change your mind, take the decision that you deem most opportune ... I tell you that because as a general rule, grenadiers are not very fond of bureaucratic tasks, and it could be that you have behaved somewhat hastily. If your companions prefer to go with them when they leave, do so. I'll wait for you until noon tomorrow. If you do not appear, we will continue the examinations "and the colonel let out a resigned sigh.

"I will come, my colonel" assured Rudi. My decision is well considered.

"Good boy. Goodbye then.

Rudi squared himself stiffly and went out into the street. A mixture of joy and sadness filled his being. On the one hand, the prospect of staying by Katia's side; on the other, the terrible moment when he would say goodbye to his friends and the officer, with whom until then he had shared the hardships and hardships of a tough campaign.

At lunchtime the grenadiers met at the barracks. They had to remain alert for the moment when the truck in charge of transporting them arrived. The teams were stacked in rows as was customary, and the lieutenant ran a brief review. The "feldwebel" ordered the grenadiers not to move from the surroundings. A motorized liaison arrived around midafternoon asking for the grenadier Rudi Mainz. He had the transfer order from Headquarters. Rudi read it and then clenched it with his fist. A tempest raged in his soul. He walked around the house in a state of tremendous tension. It all depended on a single word. The lieutenant and his two friends already knew what his decision was. Perhaps it would be better to disappear without saying goodbye. Later he would justify his attitude with a short letter. The other grenadiers knew nothing.

He saw how everyone was busy cleaning their weapon. He wouldn't have to do it anymore. His "submachine gun" would be delivered to the warehouse. Why did he want such a deadly weapon in that city where only countrymen and soldiers on leave circulated? He thought of Katia, but the figure of the young woman was now blurred in his brain, as if it belonged to the past.

He imagined his life in the office, sitting at a table full of papers whose contents he would have to decipher. From time to time they might have him interrogate some prisoners. His existence would slide in the midst of a wonderful placidity. The daily routine would eventually atrophy his senses and they would only be willing to vibrate at the sight and contact of his beloved Katia. An existence of a citizen, which would have nothing or almost nothing to do with the war.

Meanwhile, his companions would continue the harsh incursions into enemy terrain. They would place explosive charges in the places arranged by the Command. They would swoop down like lions on the sentries. They would blow up forts and surprise Command posts. His nose would continually pick up the smell of gunpowder. They would crouch before the glare of the rockets and listen to the roar of artillery shells sliding over their heads to explode a little further in dazzling flames.

If he let them go, he could walk at a leisurely pace to the headquarters offices, introduce himself to the colonel, and announce that he accepted the position. The high boss would tell him the time the next morning he would start his job. Then he would go for a walk, sit in a cafe and order beer, he would calmly wait for the time to meet Katia. Tonight they could celebrate the event by having dinner together and then they could even attend a film session at the 'Soldatenheim'.

He checked his watch. It was half past six. Twilight was already very near. At that time, the work in Katia's cafe increased. He imagined her surrounded by soldiers, listening to their loving words, smiling at them because it was necessary to do so, perhaps accepting their kindnesses.

With a sudden jerk he pulled the order out of his pocket. He read it again. He cast a glance toward the barracks. Some grenadiers stood at the door. He couldn't leave without at least saying goodbye to the lieutenant. Approached. The officer came and went giving some orders. Rudi walked over to him.

"My lieutenant" he said. I already have a transfer order in my pocket. My decision is made. I'll stay at headquarters. After all, my homework on it can be just as useful as on the first line.

"You know well that not, Rudi. In the first line you were essential. Here, there are more means. Sooner or later the colonel will find a soldier who knows the language of the country with the perfection that he demands. Instead, the patrol will be deprived of an invaluable element... and not only because they speak Russian, but for many other reasons. Anyway, I already told you yesterday that I did not intend to influence your mood. However, I want to tell you that if you ever regret it, we will be willing to welcome you as if nothing had happened. As if you came back from the hospital having healed a wound.

"Say goodbye to Bert and Alf. I wouldn't have the guts to do it myself. They have been for me the best comrades in the world... I don't know what they will think, but we must part ways.

"I will, Rudi. And you can be sure that both they and I take care of your situation.

The lieutenant held out his hand. Rudi shook it tightly.

"Goodbye, my lieutenant" he said saluting.

"In your place I would say ... Goodbye.

The officer turned and walked into the building. Rudi began his march towards the headquarters of the headquarters. He was leaving behind a whole life from which in other conditions, he would not have been separated for anything in the world.

He walked through the alleys almost in darkness. After a while, he came out onto one of the main avenues. At its opposite end was the building in which he would live from then on. He walked down the sidewalk in deep sadness. Suddenly he heard the sound of an engine behind him. A military truck was approaching at medium speed, dodging the carts of the native population. Through the windshield, Rudi made out the familiar face of Lieutenant Wahrenfels.

A sudden jolt shook her body, she looked at the crumpled paper in her hand; he stiffened. Suddenly he raised an arm. The truck slowed down.

"Wait for me! "shout.

The lieutenant was smiling. He braked the vehicle. Rudi ran like a man possessed. He jumped up and got into the back.

"Where were you? "A grenadier told him." We thought you were lost.

"I was ready," Rudi replied as the truck started up again. But I have found my way again.

The truck got smaller in the distance, wrapped in a cloud of dust, on the way to the front, danger ... and glory.